# Preacher:
# Do Unto Others

ISBN-10 1-60145-058-3
ISBN-13 978-1-60145-058-6



Printed in the United States of America.



Booklocker.com, Inc.
2006

This book and others by V. Shurtz may also be ordered through UnitedBikers.org

# Preacher:
# Do Unto Others

Book one in a series by **V.Shurtz**

***Comments:***

“A good western book that replaces the cowboys with bikers.
—Cathy Brownfield

“It made me laugh and it made me cry.” —Jackie Middleton

“A fast read.” —Danny Knight

“Exciting western-style novel.” —Berry Hill

“I liked the honesty and the sense of honor it depicted.”
—Yvonne Alexander

## *Acknowledgments*

This is to thank all of my team for making this book possible.

The country between Fallon and Ely, Nevada, Highway 50, is flat with a couple of rolling hills to break the monotony, and it's also a place where the wind in your face can take control.

In mid-May, the country is a profusion of colors and smells. If you were to notice the indigenous plants, you would feast on the golds of goldenrod, the yellows of wild mustard, and the white flower of the wild radish. The purple of vetch stands alone amongst patches of pale blue that signify lupine.

Preacher, however, was not concerned with the flowers; he was worried about the tire that was going flat!

Damn it, he thought. Where am I going to fix a flat out here?

Preacher was about fifty miles out of Fallon. Where do you find a milk crate out here?

Shit! He thought.

As he turned his head around after looking at the tire, still going flat, he saw a storefront and what looked like a gas station. The storefront became a clapboard construction, painted some sort of beige or sun-faded brown. Across the highway, the biggest cottonwood tree that Preacher had ever seen was sitting in the middle of what looked like a gravel parking lot. Through the heat waves coming from the road, the setting became clearer the closer he got. It stood out like an oasis.

The station that Preacher saw was about one hundred yards away, and he didn't know if the tire would make it that far. He crawled off the bike, with the motor still running, and started nursing the bike toward the station.

Hank stood at the base of the old cottonwood tree in front of a Texaco station. The sound of a Harley had caught his attention. It caused him to look west toward the sunset. He stared at the mirage of a warrior. He shook his head; the vision cleared and became a biker pushing his bike. Hank recognized the style. The fat bobs, the wide glide, and the throaty sound of an old '74.

Preacher saw the old man watching him as he brought his bike up to a standstill in front of one of the bay doors. The old tree was surrounded by a bench that had been built in the years past. Two trucks sat in the shade. This must be a resting spot for the locals, Preacher thought, as he took off his gloves and loosened his jacket. His black helmet sat on the sissy bar.

Around the base of the tree were a couple of old boys drinking soda, or whatever, and they were all looking at Preacher. Preacher shut off the motor, stood up, and stretched his back by arching it backwards.

"Excuse me," Preacher said, walking toward the tree, "is the owner around?"

Hank put his hands in his pockets, standard practice, prior to speaking. "That would be me," he said as he started walking forward.

"Glad to meet ya," Preacher said as he strode up to meet the hazel eyes of Hank, and offered his hand. "Preacher, Shasta County, California."

Hank looked at the offered hand. "Well, I don't know if I'm glad to meet you, but I do own this station, and if you're in need of assistance, you may be out of luck."

Preacher pulled his hand back. So that's how it's going to be, Preacher thought; okay, I can deal with this. In his most civil tone and manner, Preacher said, "Excuse me, sir, but as you can see, I have a flat tire. I was hoping that I could fix it in the shade."

Hank looked at the bike. Yup, the tire was flat. "Do you have the fixens to repair that tire? If not, I might have to charge you for the patches."

Preacher smiled, "Yeah, I've got the fixens, but I would like to rent that milk crate over to the side of the shop."

Hank smiled and looked at the milk crate beside the station. Grass was growing up through it. As he looked up, he met the gray eyes of Preacher. "Son," he said, "you're welcome to the use of that milk crate, and if you need any practice, there are a half a dozen flats next to that tire machine that need fixen, that is, if you're of a mind to."

Preacher smiled as Hank turned his back and headed back to his cronies around the tree. He had seen his type before. One of the good old boys that acted grumpy. Most would see through it.

Slapping his gloves in his left hand, Preacher turned on his heel and strode into the sunset toward his bike. It was a '71 FLH originally: wide glide, bucket headlight, and fat bobs that would take you two hundred miles. Preacher had modified it to his height and to the length of his legs. His old girl was stretched one inch with six-inch over tubes on a twenty-one inch Avon. Ape Hangers finished off the triangle with grips that were tasseled with eight inches of leather on the end. The bike was black in color with a luminance of the paint that made it look like a dark rainbow in the sun.

As Preacher walked back to the bike, he took in the bays of the station. The first one, the one closest to the office and bathrooms, had a hydraulic rack that ran off of air pressure. The other side looked like a hodgepodge of flat tires, a soak tank, and oil drums. A path of sorts weaved its way through the collection.

The outside of the station was stucco, brown with dust to gray at grass level because of the years of accumulated grease. The milk crate stood next to one of the oil barrels outside the building. Last year's grass looked like straw sticking out of everywhere.

In the front of the second bay, Preacher saw a place he could nose his bike in. The soak tank was close, and the sun was going down, so inside was a good thing. Preacher took off his jacket, set it on the tire machine with his gloves, and walked to his bike to push it forward out of the sun.

He made sure the bike was somewhat level before he went outside to retrieve the milk crate. God bless steel milk crates, Preacher thought, as he pulled it from the grass; they don't build them like this anymore. He pulled the grass out and banged the crate on the dirt. With milk crate in tow, Preacher started back to the bay.

* * * * * * *

The crew at the tree changed two or three times before Preacher got his tire fixed. Hank, however, had been watching the Preacher go about his business. In his cut-off T-shirt, Preacher had moved his bike into the bay out of the sun. As Hank watched, Preacher picked up the back of his bike, by the fender mounts, and kicked the milk crate under the frame. His shoulders and forearm muscles rippled as he worked, making his tattoos move as if they were alive. When Preacher pulled his spoons out of his saddle bags, Hank smiled and thought to himself, that man knows what he is doing.

Preacher stood up from putting his tools back in his tool pouch and looked at the sun. He had noticed Hank watching him throughout the afternoon and knew he had earned some respect from the old man. He blinked against the sun and looked back at Hank.

Hank stood looking at Preacher.

"Hank," Preacher said, "do you think I could pitch my tent next to the shop and head out in the morning?"

Hank sauntered over, stuck his hands in his pockets, and looked at Preacher with a smug look.

"Preacher," he said, "I will rent ya that space for the night and even buy ya supper over at the diner if you will fix those two split rims for me—them bastards hurt me every time."

Hank looked sideways at Preacher, "I hear they're serving meat loaf, mashed potatoes and gravy."

Preacher cocked his head, looked at the diner then back at Hank, smiled, and stuck out his hand.

"Hank, I think I could wrap myself around a good meat loaf," Preacher said.

This time Hank took the offered hand.

* * * * * * *

Maggie had been wiping down booths and tables when she heard the Harley. The sound was not that familiar out here in the middle of nowhere. Here, most traffic sounds were pick-ups and big rigs trying to beat the scales. Pulling the curtains aside, she glanced out the window. A biker was nursing his Harley up to

Hank's station with what looked like a flat back tire. This ought to give them boys something to talk about, she thought.

Maggie had grown up in this little spot in the road. Her mother had owned this diner for as long as she could remember. The diner, station, and a small store/beer bar were the focal points of this country. The ranchers and the boys around the tree had been supporting this area for years. When you're the only spot in town, everybody knows everybody.

Maggie was a good looking woman of about forty. Running the diner had kept her in shape. Standing 5'6" or 7", she had long shapely legs, a trim waist, a nice small bubble butt, and coffee cup sized breasts. Her hair was piled on top of her head in some sort of bun, and it was flaming red. She looked like Reba McEntire.

As she stood looking out at the events around the tree, she shook her head and smiled. "Well, Hank, here's your broken wing," she said to an empty room.

"Did you say something?" came a voice from the kitchen.

"It looks like your dad has a new friend," Maggie said as she dropped the curtain and started toward the counter.

The diner had three booths under the front windows. They were the old vinyl type with the table running between twin benches. Against the side wall were half a dozen tables with chairs, and a gleaming white counter with stools on chrome pedestals shone under the lights of the opposite wall.

Maggie had taken over the diner from her aged mother. She had a brisk coffee club business, which Hank was a member of, a fair lunch, and once a week she cooked a special. Her specials ran from barbecue ribs to fried chicken. Tonight it was meat loaf.

Tina came out from the kitchen, behind the counter. "What did you say? My dad has a friend?"

Maggie met her halfway between the booths and the counter. She looked back at the windows, "Yup, your dad has a friend, and the boys around the tree are going to be talking about it for a week." Maggie looked back at Tina and said, "I don't know who I feel the sorriest for, you and me for having to listen to them or that biker for having to deal with them."

Tina walked over to the windows and looked out. "Well, Dad's walking back to the tree, and the biker is walking toward his bike, so it can't be all that bad."

"Yeah, well, your dad's famous for taking in broken wings. I'm surprised he doesn't get burned more often than he does," Maggie said.

* * * * * * *

Preacher turned around after shaking Hank's hand, to survey the mess around the tire machine. Several tires stood or lay, side by side in front of the old thing. The retractor on the bottom seemed to work as Preacher stepped on the foot valve. Other than that, it would be all muscle and iron to take the tire off.

Preacher looked at the two tires Hank had indicated; the first two in the row were 7.50 x 16's on split rims. The tread on both tires and the rims matched, telling Preacher that they belonged to the same truck. Not much mud, but Preacher could see the goatheads sticking out of the rubber. There's the culprit, he thought. He rolled one out and looked around for some tools. He found what he was looking for toward the back of the shop next to an old bubble tire balancer. The hammer Preacher chose was about the size of a four-pound single jack except it had a fin on one side that looked like an adze. The next tool he looked for was an old friend, the milk crate. He found the soap in a can by the tire machine and went to work.

Preacher broke the ring loose from the rim, walked it off with a pair of long screwdrivers and looked to see if it had a boot in the tire; it did. He picked up the tire and set it down on the tire machine, spun the collar down tight, stepped on the foot valve, and broke the bottom bead loose. He spun off the collar, picked up the tire, turned it over, and dropped the tire on the milk crate. When the rim collided with the crate, the tire came loose all around. All he had to do now was push the stem through, and the tire was off. Then, it was fix the tube and put it back together.

The compressor was on the west wall of the second bay next to the dunk tank. Preacher started to fill the tube with air then stuck it in the tank. When he noticed the bubbles coming up from the tube, Preacher put his finger on it and stood up. As he did, he saw a BMX bicycle leaning against the wall. Its front tire was flat. I'm surprised Hank didn't ask me to fix that tire as well, Preacher thought. He chuckled at the idea.

* * * * * * *

As Preacher started on the second tire, he noticed a newer Ford truck pull up. A small boy, of about six, jumped out and came flying toward the station.

"Grandpa...Grandpa!" the child yelled excitedly, "I rode the mutton; I really rode the mutton." He puffed out his chest and said, "I'm going to win that mutton bustin' contest at the rodeo." Beaming with excitement and pride, the boy strutted back up to the driver of the truck. "Roy said nobody can beat me if I stick like glue. Ain't that right, Roy?"

"Isn't," Roy said, "and yup, if you stick like glue you can't be beat."

Roy wasn't a big man. He stood only about 5'10" or so with the slight build of somebody that spent a lot of time on the back of a horse. He had narrow hips, square shoulders, and forearms that rippled when he flexed his hands. His Levi shirt matched his jeans. His brown boots had seen a lot of wear. The boy was all but the spittin' image of the man, down to the small boots that he wore.

"Roy," Hank said, "Tina's going to be mad as hell at you for bringing Josh back this late."

"I suspect you're right about that, but Josh wanted to try it one last time. It was that last ride that Josh stuck for the time," Roy said. His voice wasn't apologetic, but it was that of accomplishment.

"Well you'd best explain that to his mother," Hank said.

"I think I'd rather get in a fist fight than do that," Roy said. "She doesn't think that highly of me anyway."

"Give her time, Roy," Hank said in a patient voice.

"I'd give her all the time in the world if she'd have me, but I think the devil will be selling snow cones before that happens."

* * * * * * *

While Hank and Roy were talking, Josh had wandered over to look at Preacher's bike.

"This your bike, mister?" he asked.

Preacher looked up and smiled at the boy. "Yup," he said, "that's my bike."

"Cool," Josh said. "Can I look at it?"

"Sure," Preacher said, "but remember the rule—you can look, but don't touch."

"That's what Grandpa says too," Josh said as he walked over to the bike. Look, but don't touch, and keep your hands in your pockets."

"I have a bike too," he said. "It's that one over on the wall, but it has a flat."

"I noticed," Preacher said as he went back to work on the tire.

This boy has been taught respect for other people's property, Preacher thought.

The boy was about as tall as a yard stick with dark brown hair cut short, and not as slight of build as Preacher had thought. He was a tight little bundle of muscle and sinew. This boy runs free and plays hard, Preacher thought.

"Are you working for Grandpa?" Josh asked, walking back from Preacher's bike.

"Only for a meal," Preacher said.

"Yeah," Josh said. "Grandpa does that a lot."

"We're eating over at the diner tonight too. My mom said we're having meat loaf and taters. Do you like meat loaf?" Josh asked.

"Yup," Preacher said.

"Me too; okay...we'll...see ya later," Josh said as he walked over to Hank and Roy by the tree.

About the time Josh got back to the truck, the front door to the diner opened, and a young woman of about twenty-five or so purposely walked out and crossed the highway. Preacher was patching the tube on the second tire when he heard Josh call out in an excited voice, "Mom, Mom, I rode the mutton; I rode the mutton!"

"You did?" the woman asked.

"Yup, and Roy said if I stick like glue, I'll win at the rodeo."

"That's good," she said. "Now go over to the house and get cleaned up; you're eating at the diner tonight, so get!"

"Okay," Josh said dejectedly.

"Can you pick me up tomorrow afternoon?" Josh looked expectedly at Roy.

"We'll see," Roy said as he looked at the woman.

"Josh, go get cleaned up like I told you to," his mother said.

"As for riding sheep tomorrow, or anytime soon, that will depend on what Roy has to say about being so totally irresponsible about getting you home on time," she said.

"Tina, being late was not Josh's fault. He rode for time today, and he stuck," Roy said defensively.

"I'll stick you if you don't start keeping your word. He was supposed to be home an hour ago."

Preacher looked up from the tube and smiled. Nothing like a domestic squabble to entertain one's self, Preacher thought as he took in the scene.

Tina was all of 5'4", well proportioned, with dark hair cut pixie style, and an attitude.

"Now, Tina," Roy said, "that kid has his heart set on winning at the rodeo. If you don't let him practice he won't win, damn it."

"So, now you're telling me how to raise my boy," she said in a slightly raised voice that dripped with venom.

"All I'm saying is, that boy needs a man around to help raise him, and I've taken on the chore."

"What am I, chopped liver?" Hank asked almost to himself.

"Hank, you know that's not what I meant," Roy said in an exasperated voice. "I didn't mean that at all." Looking back at Tina, he said, "All I'm saying is the kid needs a younger man to do the things he wants to do like ride bikes and ride sheep."

"Well, if you think you're going to be his daddy, you've got another thing coming, cause it ain't gonna be you," Tina said.

"Isn't," Roy said as he headed toward his truck.

"Fuck you, Roy Gene," Tina said.

Roy didn't even turn around as he said over his shoulder, "I'll pick him up at one o'clock tomorrow and *will* have him back by five."

With that, Roy got in his truck, started the engine, and with a spray of gravel and smoking tires, the truck sprang up on the highway.

Yup, Preacher thought. Nothing like a family feud to liven things up. With that, Preacher went back to the tire.

After Roy left, Hank turned to Tina, stuck his hands in his pockets and said, "Tina, you shouldn't be so hard on Roy; he's only trying to help that boy."

"Yeah, I know, but he frustrates me every time I see him. He doesn't show me any respect, and he won't listen when I tell him what I want," Tina said.

"Then don't tell; maybe ask," Hank said; "you might try some honey instead of vinegar."

Tina shook her head, "Dad, I'm not trying to catch flies." With that, she headed back to the diner.

Hank, after watching her cross the highway, walked over to Preacher who was just finishing up the second tire. "Son, you'd better get washed up as well; we don't want to be late," he said in a sarcastic voice.

Preacher nodded knowingly at Hank and said, "I don't think I want that hellcat after me for being late."

"Neither do I," Hank said; "neither do I. Come on, Preacher; I'll show you where you can wash up."

With that said, Hank walked toward the back of the shop.

* * * * * * *

Behind the office, on the right side of the first bay, Hank stepped into a doorway and flipped the switch. The room was narrow and long. It ran behind the back office wall to what Preacher thought were the outside bathrooms, about fifteen feet. At the far end was a counter with a sink at one end. A hot plate with a small coffee pot sat on the opposite end. A small fridge was under the counter and coffee pot. A twin bed sat against the wall with a cabinet of some sort, on the back wall. A few cobwebs decorated the corners, and it needed to be swept. After the chaos of the second bay, Preacher was impressed.

"Preacher," Hank said, "there's no sense you pitchin' your tent around the side of the building when there's a decent bed right here, a hot plate for coffee, and you won't get no bugs off that mattress. You might as well put your bedroll there and be comfortable."

"Sounds like a plan to me," Preacher said.

"Soap right here, scrub brush on the sink," Hank gestured toward a black and white box of 20 Mule Team Borax.

"I'll just head on over to the house and see how Josh is cleaning up." With that, Hank walked out.

Preacher heard the bell in the office ding and looked out to see what was up. The old truck that sat at the pumps had seen better days and so had the owner. The man Hank was confronting was about thirty-five with shaggy dirty hair, dirty clothes, and a beer can in one hand.

"No," Hank said. "No more credit until you and that old man of yours pay me off."

"You'll be sorry you said that one day," the stranger said.

"Eddie, don't threaten me!" Hank said with conviction in his voice.

Preacher walked out to the front of the first bay, and with Hank's last remark stinging his ears, he asked, "Hank, everything okay?"

Hank turned around with a toothy grin on his face and said, "No need to worry, Preacher, I got this handled."

"Who's this biker trash, one of Tina's lovers?" the stranger asked.

"Now you watch your mouth!" Hank shot back. "Preacher is of no concern to you; he just happens to be a friend of the family. Now get, and don't come back unless you've got some money."

"I'll be back alright, and you're not going to like it," Eddie said. He took one last pull on his beer, threw the can in the back of the truck, and left with wretched laughter erupting from the cab.

Preacher walked up to Hank as the idiot drove off. "A friend of yours?" he asked.

"No, but like those goatheads, he's a thorn in my side. You best get washed; we're due over at the diner in a bit."

"That works for me," Preacher said and walked over to his bike.

Preacher pulled his bike back from the second bay, pushed it over to the first one, and backed it in. Shouldering his saddle bags, grabbing his bedroll and poncho liner, Preacher headed toward the room that Hank had offered.

* * * * * * *

The sun was just setting when Preacher, Josh, and Hank walked across the highway to the diner. Several trucks and a few cars were parked, at various angles, in front of and alongside the place called *Maggie's*.

"It looks like Maggie's meat loaf is highly thought of around here," Preacher said as he stepped up on the porch.

"She has a better turnout for her fried chicken," Hank said, "but the meat loaf is a good standby."

Josh held the door while Hank walked in, and Preacher held the door for Josh. "Are you gonna sit with us tonight, Preacher?" Josh asked as they walked in.

"I will if you want me to," Preacher said.

"Okay," relayed Josh.

As Preacher walked through the door, he immediately stepped to the right, putting his back to the wall, and surveyed the crowd. There weren't as many customers as Preacher expected, judging from the number of cars parked outside.

The front booths were full, three tables were occupied, and two men sat at the counter.

Josh scurried over to the counter and hollered, "Mom, we're here!"

"Okay, honey," came a voice from the kitchen. "Go sit with Grandpa. I'll be right there."

"Mom, can I have a soda with supper?"

Tina stuck her head around the corner and asked, "How many did you have with Roy this afternoon?"

"Maybe a couple," he said.

"Maybe a couple, or a couple?"

"Two," Josh said.

"Then it's milk tonight," Tina said as she slipped back into the kitchen. "Go sit down, Josh, I'll be there in a minute."

"Okay," he said as he turned back toward Hank.

Preacher stood with his back to the wall as he watched Hank say "hello's" and Josh get "no's." He had washed the tire grime off himself, brushed out his long hair, and had it tied back in a pony tail that reached below his shoulder blades. He had changed Levi's and wore a Hells Angels support T-shirt with the sleeves cut off.

Preacher stood six feet tall, broad shoulders, thick chest, and had the narrow hips of a rider. Black stubble shadowed his face, and the creases around his eyes were from both laughter and squinting into the sun. There was a noticeable lull in the noise as the customers took in the stranger.

"Josh, let's sit at that first table. Preacher, pick a chair and please sit down; you're making all these cowboys nervous," Hank said with laughter in his voice.

Preacher sat with his back to the wall. He had a clear view of the entire room and the front door. It pays to be cautious in a strange environment. The tables were set for four, and the booths were set for two. Preacher glanced around the room. The walls were painted off-white with a brown border at ceiling level. The tiles on the floor were multi-colored brown to match the border. The smells emanating from the kitchen were that of fresh baked bread, meat loaf, and coffee. Preacher's stomach started to rumble. Hank came striding back to the table after sticking his head into the kitchen.

"Well, Preacher, what do ya think?" he asked as he sat down facing Preacher.

"Not as crowded as I thought it would be, judging from the trucks outside."

"Well, it's not fried chicken, but people around here do like meat loaf with gravy," Hank said. "I asked Maggie to add another slice to your plate for the work you done for me this afternoon."

"Good," said Preacher. "My stomach thinks my throat's been cut."

"Okay, you three, what do you want to drink?" Tina asked as she carried three full water glasses to the table. "Milk for Josh, coffee for Dad, and what will it be for you, Preacher—beer or coffee?"

"I think I'll stay with water, if you don't mind."

"I don't mind," said Tina.

"How did you know my name?" Preacher asked.

"Well, when Dad hollered your name out, we were all introduced to you. Besides, I saw you working over at the station this afternoon."

"That'll do," Preacher said.

"Thank you," she said as she made eye contact with Preacher. "I'll be right back."

When the plates arrived, Preacher noticed that Josh's had one piece of meat loaf, Hank's had two, and Preacher's had three thick juicy slices. His plate was piled high with whipped potatoes, and a spoon full of mixed vegetables garnished the side. The meat loaf and potatoes were swimming in rich brown gravy, and four warm homemade biscuits sat invitingly on a separate plate.

"This looks like my mama's cooking," Preacher said as Tina set the plates down.

"That's cause it *is* homemade, right down to the biscuits; enjoy," Tina said as she walked away.

* * * * * * *

It was dark when Preacher and Hank wandered out of the diner and crossed the highway over to the station. Their meal had been a relatively quiet affair. Hank had talked with his neighbors; Josh and Preacher had concentrated on the food. Maggie personally delivered the dessert of cherry cobbler with vanilla ice cream.

"Hank," Preacher said, "that was a fine meal; thank you."

"After the work you done for me this afternoon, it's the least I could do," Hank replied.

Preacher nodded his head in a silent acknowledgement. "Ya know, that Maggie's a fine lookin' woman," Preacher said; "she spoken for?"

"Naw," replied Hank. "She grew up around here, in that house behind the diner. She left right after high school, went to Reno and thought she could get a job there with one of the shows. When her momma got sick, she came home to run the diner and look after her. She's been back about five years now. I brought Tina and Josh home about three years ago, and the two of them have turned that diner into a gold mine. She does a good breakfast trade and a fair lunch, but her evenings have always been slow. It cost her more to keep the lights on and the grill hot than she was makin'. Now she closes around six, except on *special's* night. Then she stays open till the customers leave, somewhere around nine."

"I'm surprised someone hasn't gotten a hold of her, her being a good business woman," Preacher replied.

"That red hair of hers tells you a lot about Maggie; she won't have anybody. The man that can tame her will have a fine person to stand beside him."

The two of them had reached the station. Hank turned on the office lights. "Preacher, there's an enclosed shower out that back door if you're so inclined, hot water and all."

"You saying I need a shower, old man?"

"Not yet," Hank chuckled, "but if you're going to do any work tomorrow, you might."

"Work tomorrow?" Preacher asked as he turned to look at Hank with a smile on his face.

"Well, if you're not in a hurry to get gone, I could use some help over the next couple a days. Can't pay ya much, but I can sure as hell buy ya supper." Hank looked sideways at Preacher, "Can you weld?"

"Now, why would you ask me that?" Preacher asked.

"Well, Roy's dad is coming in tomorrow to pick up those two tires, and he said he has a loose muffler, and I told him we could fix it."

"Oh, you did, did ya?" Preacher chuckled.

Hank stuck his hands in his pockets as he turned to face Preacher. "Well, I sorta said I'd ask if you could weld, and if so, we would fix it. I can't see so well anymore. It's hard to use that torch if you can't see."

"What else can't you do that you need me for, Hank, more tires?"

"No," said Hank, "but I'd like to take a run into Fallon to the parts store and get some brake pads for Maggie's car. That is if you'll stay one more day."

"Well, I guess I will be needing that shower after all," Preacher replied.

"Good," Hank said. "I'll make it right for ya, Preacher."

This time Hank stuck out his hand.

* * * * * * *

Maggie and Tina were cleaning up after supper. Tina started the dishwasher and wiped off the work counters in the kitchen as Maggie wiped the tables and swept the floors.

Maggie was wiping down the counter when Tina came out from the kitchen. "Well, Maggie, what do ya think of Preacher?"

"He's big, that's for sure."

"He's good looking too," Tina said as she smiled at Maggie, "in a rugged sort of way."

"That man could cause a lot of trouble if you crossed him," Maggie said as she looked over at the station to see Hank and Preacher talking.

"Imagine, a Preacher on a shovel."

"What did you say?" Tina asked. "A Preacher on a shovel—is that anything like a witch on a broom?"

"Not even the same, Tina," Maggie said.

"A shovel is a type of motor for that Harley. It's an old '74 by the looks of it."

Tina stopped at the corner of the counter and looked at Maggie. With an evil grin on her face, she asked, "Now, how would you know that, Maggie?"

Maggie looked back at Tina, wiggled her eyebrows and simply said, "History, girl, history."

They both exploded with laughter.

* * * * * * *

Preacher wasn't ready to go to bed when he finished laying out his bedroll and poncho liner. He made the coffee for tomorrow with grounds out of his saddle bags and then pulled out his medicine. He knew it was against the law to have cannabis in Nevada, but it helped him relax. With swift adept hands, he rolled a joint and stuck it behind his ear. His bike was resting comfortably in the first stall. Grabbing a clean rag off the workbench against the back wall, he started wiping the old girl down—five hundred pounds of black paint, chrome, and steel. When he finished, he folded the rag and laid it on the seat. The light was off in the office. The only light came from Preacher's room. Let's go see this shower, Preacher said to himself.

As Preacher stepped out the back door, he could see lights on in the house off to the right and back off of the highway. The shower was an old shower stall walled in by plywood and two by fours. A short bench was built into one of the walls, and there were hooks screwed into the back of the door that enclosed the small shower room. The floor was concrete, and a single light bulb hung from the ceiling. Preacher reached up and pulled the attached string. Well, at least I have light, Preacher thought as he turned on the faucets.

And now we have water, he said to himself. After turning off the water and the light, Preacher walked out of the shower room and looked at the pipe that came out from under the concrete. Gray water—I'll bet they need that in the summer, he thought. With that, he turned the corner and headed toward the old cottonwood tree.

The night had turned chilly, not so uncommon in this high desert. To ward off any chill that might come up as night wore on, Preacher had put his cut-off jacket on before he went looking for the shower. Now, he sat with his back to the tree, on the bench that surrounded it. He lit the joint and felt the bite of the first hit.

After three tokes, he extinguished it between his fingers and put the roach in the pocket of his scrodie.

"You know that stuff is illegal in Nevada, don't ya?" Hank said as he walked in front of the station toward the tree.

"Yeah, so?" Preacher returned. "You have a problem with it, Hank?"

"No, I figure you're old enough to do as you please; only wanted to warn ya," Hank responded.

Not turning his head or moving to get up, Preacher just sat there. After a few beats, Preacher looked at Hank and responded, "Okay, I've been warned."

"You are a hard one, aren't ya, Preacher?"

"Not really; I don't mingle in other peoples' business, and I don't allow others to mingle in mine."

"I agree," said Hank, "but I do have a grandson that doesn't need to be exposed, if you know what I mean."

"I'll abide by that," Preacher stated. "I don't think any kind of smoke is good for kids, including cigarettes."

They sat silently for awhile.

"Gettin' a little chilly out tonight," Hank said.

"It's working on it," Preacher replied.

"I called Gene, that's Roy's dad, and told him you would weld that muffler for him."

"And, what did he say?" Preached asked.

"He said he would be by first thing in the morning."

"Good," Preacher said.

"You all settled in?" Hank asked.

"About as settled as I'm going to get."

"Good," said Hank as he got up. "I'll see you early then."

"How early is early?" Preacher asked as Hank started to walk away.

"Early enough to feed you breakfast and get back to the station by eight o'clock. That's when I open."

"And, you close at six; is that right?"

"About then," Hank replied. "See ya come morning." With that, Hank started toward the house.

See ya in the morning, Preacher said to the night air. He reached into his pocket for the roach.

* * * * * * *

The morning was clear and cool when Preacher walked out the back door of the station. The sun was halfway up the horizon, and it looked like it was going to be a glorious day. Behind the station stood a stack of pallets, oil barrels, and some discarded car or truck parts. The gray water line Preacher had seen the night before went into a small ravine, running east to west behind the house and station. Small cottonwoods ranged up and down the draw. While Preacher stood at the back door, a jackrabbit looked up from a small patch of green grass at the end of the pipe. With a salute of the coffee cup, Preacher acknowledged its presence.

Hank's house stood back and to the right of the station. The lawns were mowed, the roses were trimmed, and it was surrounded by the typical white picket fence. Several rabbits dined on the lush dew laden expanse of green held within the white border.

Hank had been standing at the front window, watching the sun and the rabbits. This was his favorite time of the year—cool, crisp mornings and not so hot during the day. The rabbits had alerted Hank to a stranger's presence when they stopped eating and looked, with ears straight up and forward, at the station.

"Preacher's up," Hank said.

Tina came out from the small kitchen and looked out the window to see Preacher raise his coffee cup in a salute to the rabbits. "If he's up and has already made his coffee, he's not some slacker," Tina stated matter-of-factly.

"That's what I was just thinkin'," Hank said. "The rabbits didn't run, so I guess that tells us something."

"Well, what it tells me is that I've got to go," Tina returned as she walked back to the kitchen.

"Are you going to Fallon today?" she asked from the kitchen.

"I think so," Hank said. "I don't know how long I can get Preacher to stay. He said he'd fix Gene's muffler this morning, so I think I'll leave as soon as he shows up."

"Well, if you leave, tell me."

"What do I have to do, ask your permission?" Hank asked.

"No," said Tina, "but if you're gone by eight-thirty or nine, you should be back by two or three. It's only one hundred miles or so, round trip. If you're not back by then, I'll worry."

"Well, don't send out the cavalry; I might stay and have lunch and a beer at some place other than *Maggie's*," Hank said as he walked through the kitchen and stepped out the back door.

Preacher noticed the rabbits on the lawn had stopped eating and were looking back at the house. I wonder what has got them on the lookout, Preacher thought.

Preacher heard the creak of a screen door and looked over to see Hank step out the back door. The rabbits were watching him as he started toward the station on a path that was bordered by round river rocks. The path was graveled and led to where Preacher stood at the back door. The rabbits moved off a little but didn't shy away as he expected.

This must be a morning ritual, Preacher thought as Hank came closer. The rabbits had already begun to nibble again.

As Hank walked up the path, he noticed that Preacher had shaved, and his hair was pulled back in a warrior's braid, not loose as it had been last night. He was wearing his cut-off jacket where his trip pins sparkled, reflecting the rising sun.

"Well, I see you survived," Hank said cordially.

"Yup, I did," Preacher replied.

"Good; you up for breakfast?" Hank asked.

"After that supper last night, I think I'll marry the cook," Preacher said as he turned around and walked back into the station.

"Well, I don't know about that, but Maggie does have the best biscuits and gravy you ever wrapped a lip around."

"Is she open already?" Preacher asked.

"Well, it's a little after six, so I guess we're safe to wander over," Hank replied as he walked out the front door of the station.

*Maggie's* was indeed open, and a few trucks were already lined up in the front. Hank and Preacher walked in to find the counter the place of activity. Maggie was filling coffee cups; a few of the old boys Preacher had seen yesterday were discussing anything and everything from the weather to the biker Hank had staying over at the station. In a little spot like this one, everyone knows everything.

"Good morning, Hank," she said with a smile and a wave of the coffee pot.

"Good morning, Maggie," Hank said as he wandered over to a booth.

"Coffee?" she asked.

"You bet, and some biscuits and gravy when you get the chance," Hank replied.

"How 'bout you, Preacher?" she asked.

"Same," said Preacher as he slid into the booth that was backed up to the wall.

"On its way," she said as she grabbed two coffee cups from under the counter.

"One biscuit or two?" she asked Hank as she poured their coffee.

"One," replied Hank.

"Preacher?" she asked.

"If they're anything like last night's biscuits, I'll have one with gravy and one for jelly."

"Aah," she said with a smile. "The Preacher has a sweet tooth."

"Maggie," Hank said, "I'm going into town today to get your brake pads. Do you need anything else?"

"Not that I can think of. You gonna fix the brakes today?" she asked.

"I don't think I'll get back in time, but if you can talk Preacher into staying around one more day, we'll get them done tomorrow."

Preacher looked at Hank, "Is this another way of saying, it hurts you or you can't see?"

"Preacher, if you'll help Hank with my brakes, breakfast is on me," she said as she smiled.

"What, are you two in cahoots or something? Hank buys supper for a couple of tires; now you're bribing me with breakfast to fix your brakes? I may not even know how to fix brakes," Preacher stated, sounding indignant. "I'm supposed to be at a get acquainted run in Zion Park at the end of the month."

Maggie just looked at him, smiling. "Well then, you've got plenty of time to fix my brakes and make your run," she said matter-of-factly.

"Don't I even get a vote?" Preacher asked.

Maggie and Hank looked at each other, smiled, then looked over at Preacher and said in unison, "No."

"Alright then, I guess we know who the slave is, don't we?" Preacher said. Looking up at Maggie, he continued, "This may cost more than a meal."

"Honey, don't you worry about a thing; Maggie will take care of you, if you take care of her."

"I'll just bet you could," Preacher responded.

"Count on it, Preacher; count on it." With that she was gone.

* * * * * * *

With breakfast over, Preacher and Hank said their goodbyes to Maggie and sauntered over to open the station.

"The tanks are in the back of the second bay by the workbench, and there are coat hangers in that cabinet in your room," Hank said as he walked into the station. "After I introduce you to Roy's dad, I'm going into Fallon to get those brakes for Maggie, and I should be back early this afternoon."

"Hank," Preacher said, "you understand that tomorrow or the next day I'm leaving, don't you?"

"Yeah, I understand, and I hope you understand how much I appreciate your help."

"Yeah, well, don't get accustomed to me being here."

"Preacher, you're free to leave now if you want, but I've never met a man of your culture yet that didn't live up to his word, once it's given."

"Now you're stroking me."

"No, I'm not; I just can't imagine you, of all people, backin' down from a promise."

"Hank, you don't even know me."

"Oh, yes I do; your kind are hard men, Preacher, but your word is your bond."

The honk of a horn had both men turning around and looking at the old Chevy truck that had just pulled up to the bay doors.

"That'll be Gene; open the bay door, and I'll go talk to him."

Preacher opened the bay door and pushed his bike out, bringing it to rest in front of the office window so he could keep an eye on it.

* * * * * * *

Gene was an older version of Roy: same build, same height, and same mannerism. Hank guided him on the rack, then turned to Preacher and said, "Preacher, please do what you can, and I'll settle up with Gene later, okay?"

"Sure, no problem."

"No credit on gas, and there's money in the till. I'll see ya this afternoon."

Preacher nodded his head yes and set the rack to pick up the old truck.

"Preacher," Gene asked, "Could you mount those tires too?"

Preacher looked at Gene, "You old boys are all the same; sure, why not," Preacher replied. "I've got nothing better to do."

Gene followed Hank out.

"Hank, do you think it's safe to leave him here with your shop and your money?" Gene asked.

"I don't have to worry about a thing, Gene, not as long as he's here. I think that man would hurt anyone who tried to do me wrong. I've seen his type before. He won't be here long, but he will do what he says. I pity the man that crosses him," Hank stated. With that, he stuck his head in the bay, "Preacher, I'll see ya this afternoon."

Preacher just nodded.

* * * * * * *

Preacher finished Gene's truck about the time the old man returned from across the highway. Two tailpipe hangers, one donut gasket, and about twenty minutes of welding had the truck back on the road with the spare tires in the bed.

Gene hadn't said a word to Preacher before he went to breakfast. Preacher had heard what Hank said prior to leaving for Fallon. The trust Hank had in him, had him wanting to prove that that trust was not unwarranted.

Now, as the morning was winding down, Preacher took the time to push his bike back to the first bay, and using the milk crate for a stool, he adjusted his valves. Preacher had invented a little tool that had the distance between the locknut and the pushrod head, welded to a stem of #9 wire. The gauge was chrome and came in handy if you had a hot motor, but if the motor was cold, it always was a good idea to go by the book and bottom out the lifter then back up to adjust the rod. The job was not that hard, but if you had hydraulic lifters, it was a continual one. Once the motor was back to normal, Preacher started cleaning.

Shasta County, California had only been about six hours prior to the flat tire, and Hank. Now, Preacher was thinking about the reasons he had left: a sticky divorce, a bankruptcy, and a one dollar super lotto ticket that had netted him twenty-four million after taxes. A lawyer friend and fellow motorcycle enthusiast had helped Preacher tuck his money away in several interest bearing accounts. He had also suggested a separate account that Preacher could draw from when the need required him to. Once the money was put away and working, Preacher had decided it was time to clear away any cobwebs of the mind and decide what he wanted to do for the rest of his life. It was time for a ride. Preacher's father had left him a few acres that Preacher had moved a trailer on after the divorce, and that was all the ties Preacher had to his past life.

It was definitely time for a ride—where? Wherever it takes me, Preacher thought as the bell, signifying another customer, rang. Preacher stood to take care of them.

The ranchers and about half of the state of Nevada had come to Hank's to buy gas and look at the biker Hank had trusted to run the station. Most had been polite, and Preacher had treated them with courtesy. Some of the old boys were out at the tree, and all were waiting for Preacher to do something—to do what? Preacher couldn't imagine—rape and maim, plunder and pillage? Anticipation was felt from the very air that surrounded them.

Tina had come home after the breakfast rush, and now Maggie was walking across the highway.

"Preacher," she inquired, "Are you going to want a meat loaf sandwich for lunch?"

"Are you still bribing me?" Preacher asked.

"No; Hank said he would buy lunch if you were so inclined."

"Well, in that case, yes, I would like a sandwich with extra mayo and sweet pickle relish if you would, please."

"Still have that sweet tooth, Preacher?"

"Had it all my life," he responded.

"How are you getting along over here?" she asked.

"So far so good, what with all the friends and neighbors coming by for five dollars of gas, I'll bet Hank'll make a good profit today," he replied.

"Preacher," she said, "Hank's one of the good old boys around here, and he's always helping somebody. You just happen to be the current novelty."

"Yeah, well, this novelty will be gone tomorrow, so they better get a good look."

Maggie chuckled, "I have a feeling these old boys will be talking about you for a long time after you're gone."

"Let's hope that when they talk, they say something good. Most people think people like me are outlaws, and that's just not so. Bikers just ride a different kind of horse, that's all."

"You don't have to tell me, Preacher, I've been around your kind most of my adult life," Maggie stated.

Preacher looked sideways at Maggie, "I don't think you know me at all," he said.

"Don't be surprised, Preacher; don't be surprised." With that, she headed back to the diner.

Preacher watched her as she strode across the highway. The rear view was just as pleasant as the front. Preacher did have an appreciation for a good hard female body, and the one walking away was definitely eye candy.

* * * * * * *

Preacher was leaning back in the chair behind the desk in Hank's office area. He had just finished the lunch Maggie had delivered: a meat loaf sandwich, extra mayo with sweet pickle relish, a huge scoop of the best potato salad Preacher had eaten in a while, and a large frosty mug of iced tea with lemon.

If Hank gets back in time, I could do Maggie's brakes this afternoon and be gone with the sunrise, he thought. Being the center of attention was wearing his nerves to a raw edge.

The sound of Roy's voice had Preacher looking over to the big cottonwood. Roy stood amongst the old boy crowd, shaking hands and smiling. He had started over toward the station when a six-year-old streak of black hair came flying across the front window to slide to a halt about ten feet in front of him.

"We going to ride this afternoon, Roy?" Josh asked.

"Well, I'm not here for my good looks," Roy responded. "Miguel brought in another herd of sheep last night, and we've been culling them all morning. All of these are range animals, and there's one old black ram. I'd say if you could ride him and stick, you will win at the rodeo."

"Yes!" Josh said enthusiastically. "I'll go and tell Mom and then be right back, okay?"

"Okay," Roy was smiling when he walked into the office.

"Preacher, I want to thank you for takin' care of Dad this morning."

"Not a problem," Preacher replied. "All it took was a donut gasket, a couple of tailpipe hangers, and that old Chevy was good as new."

"Dad sets store by that old truck. He was surprised that you fixed it as fast as you did."

"Yeah, well, those old Chevy's are easy to work on."

"Well, you can bet that old Hank gets told how much Dad appreciated what you did for him," Roy said.

"I think Hank will hear a lot of things when he gets back," responded Preacher.

"Yeah, well, the boys out at the ranch even know you're here."

"From the amount of five dollar sales at the gas pump, I'd say half of the valley knows I'm here."

"Most people around here aren't used to a real biker in amongst 'em. I'd say you have become the main event around here."

"I don't want to be the main event anywhere," Preacher said half to himself.

"Like it or not, that's the way it goes in this valley," Roy stated. "When do you expect Hank back?"

"He told me he would be back this afternoon."

"Good," Roy said, "I'll talk to him about the bill then. See ya later, Preacher. I've got a boy that needs to practice if he's going to win at the rodeo." With that, he stepped out the front door.

* * * * * * *

The gravel road leading to Gene and Roy's ranch was six miles of dust and rabbit brush. After getting off the main road and crossing a cattle guard, fences were nonexistent. During the trip, Josh had been loquacious. He was past the *why?* stage. He now had an opinion on everything, especially mutton bustin'.

"How many sheep did you bring in? How many were culled? Do I get to ride them all? I have to practice you know. Do I get to ride the black ram?"

Roy had listened to the incessant jabbering many times. It always amused him that the little guy could carry on a conversation quite well by himself. This boy really needs a dad, he thought.

The ranch was a sprawling affair. The main house was at the end of the road. Equipment sheds and a holding pen were off to the left. A barn and small green pasture, about ten acres, were situated behind the house and sheds.

When Roy parked his truck, Josh was out the door like a shot. He ran first to the holding pen, then on to the small arena that Miguel and Roy had set up for his practice sessions.

"Where are all the sheep?" he asked.

"The culls and that old ram are in the pen behind the barn," Roy answered.

Josh was off again, heading toward the barn.

When Roy got to the pen, Josh was standing on the fence rails, gauging his future combatants.

"What do you think of this bunch?" Roy asked.

The bunch was thirteen ewes and one old roman-nosed black ram. The ram was watching Josh and Roy through black, unblinking eyes. The ewes were milling around him.

The old ram was a range animal. Human intervention and fences were not part of his normal routine.

A sheepherder on a horse with a couple of good border collies was the normal. Humans had interfered with that routine. The sheep were confused by the loss of their companions as well as the fences. The old grizzled ram had fought coyotes, worried feral dogs, and even taken on a herder or two over the years. This old boy knew what he could do to those two humans on the fence.

"Can I ride them all?" asked Josh.

"Not today," Roy responded.

"Can I ride the black one?"

"Let's see how you do with the ewes. I'll have Miguel put a couple in the chute. These are range animals, Josh; they're not the back pasture lambs you've been riding. Now, go get your helmet and mouthpiece. Your mother would kill me if you got hurt."

"Okay…I'll be right back. I'll meet you at the chute." With that, he was off.

Miguel and his dogs cut out three of the best looking ewes and herded them into the chute that led to the makeshift arena.

Miguel was the foreman of the ranch. Herding sheep out on the desert for a month at a time was a lot of hard work. When the weather was bad or the carnivores were active, the herder had to spend considerable time in the saddle. Miguel knew his business, and he knew sheep.

Miguel had watched Josh's development throughout the spring. He had to admit, the kid was a fast learner. Josh had shown both tenacity and natural talent from the start. The three ewes Miguel put in the chute were in good shape. Range animals were hardier than pasture animals. Natural selection and predation had culled the weak and the crippled. These three old ewes had survived by instinct and strength. If Josh can ride these sheep, he *will* be good enough to win at the rodeo, Miguel thought.

Josh was back before Roy and Miguel could put the cinch strap on the first old ewe.

"Are we ready yet?" he asked.

"Slow down, Josh," Roy said admonishingly. "Concentrate; think," he continued. "When you get on the back of any animal, you have to be focused."

"I know," Josh said; "think in the middle."

"That's my boy," Roy said as he scuffed the top of the helmet Josh had donned. "Okay, Josh; let's get you on the back of one of these critters."

Josh closed his eyes, clinched his small fists, and repeated the instructions he had been given every time he rode. "Think in the middle, keep your head down, hold the pad to your chest, and don't let go."

Roy picked Josh up and sat him straddle the ewe. "Get set, Josh," Roy said with anticipation.

When Josh was ready, he nodded his head.

"Now!" Roy yelled, and Miguel opened the gate.

The sheep went out like a shot, made a beeline for the far fence and spun to the left. Confused, the ewe didn't know what to do or where to go. As she slowed down, Josh kicked off, landing on his feet.

"That's it, son; you did it!" Roy howled.

"Yes," Josh said as he brought his small fist down like a referee calling time.

Miguel sent one of the dogs out to bring the ewe back to the pen as Josh strutted back to Roy.

"That ride will win," Roy stated.

The next two rides were almost a repeat of the first, although Josh didn't always land on his feet.

"Well, Miguel, what do you say about that old black ram; should we bring him up?"

"He is un Diablo, Señor Roy," he stated. "He is very mean. The little one maybe should not ride that one."

"Maybe you're right," Roy said thoughtfully.

"Josh," Roy yelled, "let's get some chores done. Remember, you play; you pay."

"Just one more...please," Josh begged.

"Maybe later; right now you have work to do."

The next hour was filled with cleaning stalls, hauling water, and feeding the livestock, including the sheep in the pen.

Miguel had just come in from looking at the flock and was talking with the herder.

Josh was putting the wheelbarrow away when Roy walked into the barn. "Josh, are you through yet?"

"I just finished," Josh said.

"You're a good kid, Josh. Having you around makes me want a son of my own," Roy said.

"I'll be your son. Living with you would be fun."

"Even with all the work?" Roy asked.

"I like the work, and I could ride whenever I wanted," Josh responded excitedly.

"Only after the work's done," Roy admonished.

"Can I ride one more time today?" Josh asked.

"You've done your work; we have an hour before I have to get you back...yes, one more time."

"Miguel!" Roy hollered, "let's give Josh one more ride. Bring up that old ram."

"Are you sure?" Miguel asked.

"I think it will be okay, if we keep those dogs handy," Roy said.

"As you say," Miguel muttered as he walked over to the pen to bring up the old black devil.

"Now Josh, this old guy is mean. So, if you get thrown, tuck your head, and roll away from him. Miguel and I will have the dogs ready to get him away from you. Don't get up until I tell you to, okay?"

"Okay," Josh said.

Josh put on his helmet and pulled the chin strap tight.

The ram was not coming up quietly. He was banging against the rails, and his nose was running. The dogs ran him up to the gate, and Roy slipped a pole behind his rump. Miguel swung the cinch under his chest, and Roy secured it in place.

"Remember, Josh, think in the middle, head down, and if you get thrown, roll and stay down until the dogs can get him out of there."

"Okay," Josh said.

Roy could tell the kid was focused and ready. As Roy set the boy straddle the old ram, he kicked out with his back hooves and swung his head from side to side.

"Ready, Josh?"

With a nod Miguel opened the gate.

The ram came out of that chute like he was fired from a cannon. Like the ewes, he ran straight at the fence. The rails bowed when he slammed into them. Josh flew off the ram's back, and when his head hit the fence it sounded like a melon hitting concrete. Miguel turned the dogs loose immediately. Josh was lying in a heap, not moving.

Roy was running before Josh hit the ground. Dear God, don't let my boy be hurt, he thought. With tears in his eyes, Roy slid on his knees up to Josh. His right arm was at an odd angle, and blood trickled out of his small nose. Josh was unconscious.

* * * * * * *

Preacher had spent the rest of the afternoon cleaning. Between the gas purchases and the gawkers, it had been interesting. News must travel fast out here, Preacher thought. Preacher had become the local novelty. He was more amused than irritated with the procession.

Preacher had swept out the office, cleaned off the workbench, and was in the process of cleaning the first bay when Hank finally returned from his day in the city. Preacher glanced up when the bell sounded to see Hank pulling up to the front of the station. The crowd around the tree called out greetings when Hank finally got out of the truck. Hank walked over to greet his cronies and get the report he knew was coming.

Preacher knew what was transpiring over at the tree. The thought of what was to be said made him chuckle.

"Sounds like you've had a busy day today," Hank said to Preacher when he returned from the tree.

"Not really," Preacher said.

"I worked on my bike, ate lunch, and now I'm cleaning up so I can get to those brakes," he continued. "I was thinking, if I could get to them this afternoon, I could be gone with the sunrise."

"If that's what you want, I don't have a problem with it," Hank stated. "What's your hurry?"

"No hurry," Preacher said; "when I left Shasta County I was looking to get my head on straight, not spend my time welding and fixin' tires. I told you I would help because you helped me yesterday. With these brakes, I think we're square."

"More than square," Preacher," Hank said dejectedly. "So, you're off to Zion Park then?"

"That's just the first stop; I don't know where I'm going after that," Preacher said.

"You're just going and don't know where?" Hank asked.

"That's about the size of it," replied Preacher.

"That's why most people don't understand your type, Preacher. Most people couldn't just pack up and go with no destination. That kind of freedom would scare them."

"I'm not most people," said Preacher.

"That you're not, Preacher."

"Here's the work order for Gene: two tailpipe hangers, a donut gasket, and twenty minutes of welding. Roy said he would pay when he saw you."

"Good, good," Hank responded.

Hank looked up at Preacher and asked, "You sure you want to do those brakes this afternoon? It's after four o'clock already, and it might take a couple of hours to get them done."

"I'd like to be gone by sunrise tomorrow, Hank," Preacher said assertively.

"Then I guess I better walk over and get Maggie's car. The brake pads are in the truck."

As Hank turned to leave the office, Tina came flying out the front door of *Maggie's*. She had tears on her cheeks, and she ran up to Hank. "Dad," she pleaded, "you've got to take me to Reno—now!"

"Hold on, young lady, what's happened?"

"Josh has been hurt, and they airlifted him from Gene's ranch to Washoe Trauma Center. We have to go, now!" she screamed.

Hank looked at Preacher, "Preacher?"

"Go," Preacher said, "go."

Hank jumped back in the truck and started it as Tina climbed in.

"Preacher, I owe ya," Hank said out the driver's window.

"You're right," Preacher said accepting the situation. "I hope the kid's okay; now go, before I change my mind."

"Thanks, Preacher," Hank replied.

Preacher looked over at *Maggie's* to see her standing on the porch. He looked back to see Hank's truck going west into the sun and wondered when they might be back.

Shit! he thought. Now what have I gotten in the middle of? He recalled a cliché. No good deed goes unpunished.

* * * * * * *

Preacher stood in the afternoon sun, watching Hank's truck disappear down the highway. No good deed goes unpunished was echoing in his mind. Here I am, he thought, standing in the middle of bum-fuck Egypt, with my dick in my hand, and I should be past Ely on my way to I-15! Shit, he said to himself.

Footsteps crunching on gravel made Preacher turn toward the sound as Maggie was walking up behind him with a worried look on her face. "I hope Josh is okay," she said.

"Me too," Preacher responded.

After a moment's pause, Maggie continued, "Well, Preacher, I guess you've been elevated up from novelty to history with this accident."

"What do you mean by that?" he asked in a hard tone.

"Yesterday, you pulled up to Hank's with a flat tire, stayed for supper, fixed Gene's truck, watched the station for Hank so he could go to town, and now here you are saving the day by staying while Hank and Tina deal with an emergency. This story will be told by three generations: Hank, Tina, and Josh. You're one of the main characters, and that makes you history."

"I don't want to be history. I should be on my way. I should be at the junction of Highway 50 and I-15, wondering if I should turn right to Zion or left to Salt Lake, but, nooo...here I am stuck in bum-fuck waiting for an old man to get back."

"Preacher," she said in an earnest voice, "you couldn't leave Hank hanging anymore than you could wish harm on that little boy. You did the right thing."

"Is that supposed to make me feel better?"

Her voice turned flippant. "I don't care if it does or doesn't. The fact still stands. Besides, you still have to fix my brakes."

"I don't have to do anything," he snapped. "I could get on that bike and leave right now, and there's nothing you or anybody else could do about it."

"Okay, Preacher, if that's the way you feel," she said in a new hard voice. "Here's the deal: I'm out a waitress, and you're out a day or two. I won't be your mouse, but I will feed you."

Preacher had to smile at Maggie's straightforward talk. He liked this woman.

"Fuck you," he replied softly.

Maggie smiled as she bumped him with her hip. "Stick around here long enough, you just might get the chance." With that, she started back across the highway.

* * * * * * *

Tina was silent for the first few miles. Hank knew his daughter. She would get over the shock first and then get mad. Almost as if on cue, Tina started in a quiet voice, reaching a crescendo, "If that son-of-a-bitch hurt my boy, I'm going to kill him! And he thinks he wants to be that boy's father? I don't think so. He can't even take care of himself, let alone my boy. What was he thinking?"

"Tina," Hank ventured, "what happened?"

"Josh cracked his head on a fence post; that's what happened. Roy put him on an old ram, and he hit his head on the fence when the ram ran into it." Now in a low voice, Tina muttered, "I'm going to kill him; I'm going to kill him."

"Tina, it sounds like an accident to me. Give the man a chance. All he has ever tried to do was be a father figure for that boy, and I think Josh needs that."

"Think what you want," Tina returned; "just drive."

Hank shook his head. This is going to be a long two hours, he thought. He knew Tina would internalize this until they reached the hospital, then he'd better get in between her and Roy.

Preacher was still irritated over the whole situation. He had tried to help Hank because he had helped him. Now, he was stuck because of an accident. Accidents are just that—accidents. To be mad at Hank was unreasonable. Hank had done nothing but be kind. The old man has heart, Preacher thought, and a good heart is what had kept him at the station for the second time today.

Preacher shook his head as he slowly walked back to the station office. Hank had left the brake shoes for Maggie's car on the desk. When Preacher looked at the boxes, he couldn't help but think of the red haired woman. He had confronted her type before. She could be a good friend or your worst nightmare. As a lover, she would probably be very energetic, and that made Preacher smile.

Looking around, he decided that flat tires would work off some of the anxiety he had been feeling. He ran his hand gently over the big black bike that rested in the first bay as he strolled over to the tire machine.

Looking down at the stack, or row, of tires to be fixed, his mind calculated the time. It would probably take two hours to fix them all. He looked around the second bay. Tomorrow was another day, and it would be as boring as today. The tires would wait. His eyes had settled on a blue BMX bicycle with a flat tire. Now that is a tire I can fix and make a difference. He smiled at the thought. Purposefully, he walked over, picked up the bike and inverted it so it rested on the seat and handle bars. This one's for the boy. I don't think he'll be riding sheep for a while.

After Maggie left Preacher standing at the station, she thought about him a lot. He is a good man, she thought, and he's helping even though he could leave. He's not happy, but he will do what he said, and that says a lot about a man. If he's going to be part of this town's history, she wanted to be part of his. Call it community service; call it a thank you; call it a gift.

He had just finished putting the bike back together when a 1969 Malibu SS pulled up to the first bay. The glowing deep forest green paint was complemented by a glistening black vinyl top. magnesium mags with Tiger Paw tires had it looking as if it could, indeed, jump up and grab you. The windows were tinted, and when Maggie rolled down the driver's side window, Preacher noticed white tuck and roll Naugahyde bucket seats.

"Hey, mister, want a ride?"

Preacher chuckled and replied, "Does it have any brakes?"

"I don't know; I never use them, but it does have an accelerator." Maggie was beaming. She had changed out of her waitress uniform and now wore a tank top, without a bra, and a pair of tight shorts that enhanced her smooth, tanned long legs. She swiveled out the door and uncoiled. "What do you think of my car?"

Preacher was walking around the Malibu, appreciating the familiar curves and lines of the classic. "Not bad, not bad at all. Where did you come by this beauty?"

"I had it built when I was in Reno."

"I'll bet that wasn't a cheap thrill."

"How much do you have tied up in that bike?"

"About the same."

"Wanna go for a ride?"

Maggie had let her hair down and brushed it out. She stood in moccasins, legs spread to shoulder width with her hands on her hips. The shorts were short, and the tanned skin of a very flat stomach accentuated the beige shorts and the white midriff tank top. Her nipples stood at attention. She knew Preacher was noticing. She had dressed for him. If they were going to be seeing each other everyday for a few days, she was going to have some fun. "Come on, Preacher, close up this station and climb in. We'll see how long it takes us to go fifty miles."

Preacher looked at Maggie, smiled, and said, "Now that's a deal I can live with." He closed and locked the bay doors. Maggie had walked in the front door as Preacher was shutting the doors and followed Preacher into his room. "So you're staying in Hank's back room," she said as she sat on the bed.

"Yup, all the amenities of home: good bed, running water, a place to park my bike, and a shower out back. It's not the Hilton, but I've stayed in a lot worse."

Maggie bounced on the bed. "The bed squeaks," she commented.

Preacher smiled as he lathered up his hands and arms. "Maggie," he said, "I don't want to be responsible for Hank's money. What would you think about keeping thirty dollars or so in the till for change, and each night I give you the rest? Hank's going to need it, with Josh in the hospital."

"That's okay with me. I'll put it in my safe until he gets back," she replied.

"Good; now let me change this shirt, and we'll see what that old Chevy can do." Preacher pulled off his T-shirt and opened his saddle bags for a clean one.

Maggie had watched Preacher as he washed up. When he mentioned the money, she sat up and listened. Not many people would think about Hank and Josh, but Preacher had. When he pulled off his shirt, Maggie felt a tingle run through her body, one she hadn't felt for a long time. His stomach was the traditional six-pack, and his shoulders were well formed. A small patch of hair centered his chest, not much, but enough.

"Where are we going?" he asked as he pulled on another Harley T-shirt.

"Just down the road a ways. There's a place east of here I'd like to show ya. It's one of my favorites. I thought as long as you're here, I might as well show you the sights."

"With you wearing that outfit, you think I'm going to be looking at the local flora and fauna?" he asked.

Maggie flushed, "Well, sometimes it's nice to have a guide when you're not familiar with the terrain."

"I can understand how a man might get lost in all those unknown peaks and valleys," he said.

"Not to worry," she said with an impish grin, "I'll guide you."

Preacher tucked in his shirt and offered her his hand to help her off the bed. When she stood, he pulled her close and looked into her green eyes. They were so close that he could see her rapid pulse under the skin of her neck. "Then guide me," he said as his hands came to rest on her hips. His lips brushed over hers. She placed the palms of her hands on his chest, but offered little resistance.

"Preacher, if we don't go soon, it'll be too late."

He looked into those deep green eyes and saw reluctance.

"Okay," he said as he grasped her hand and headed for the door. "Let's go. You can show me the birds and the bees later. Let's go look at some flowers."

Maggie was surprised by his reaction. She didn't know if she should be relieved or disappointed.

* * * * * * *

Hank and Tina arrived at Washoe around six-thirty. Hank dropped Tina off at the front doors. It took him fifteen minutes to find a parking place and walk back to the entrance.

The foyer of the hospital was an immense area filled with confusion and anxiety. All hospitals smell the same, Hank thought. Hank hated hospitals. The last time he had been in one was the day his beloved wife had passed away. Now, he was here to support his daughter and care for his grandson. He really hated hospitals. He found Tina at the information counter, waiting anxiously.

"They have him admitted, but they're not sure where." Pointing with her chin, she motioned toward a candy striper. "She's calling now."

The candy striper hung up the phone and walked over to the counter. "Ms. Kyle, your son is still in surgery. Follow those arrows," she pointed to the wall, "and they will lead you to the waiting room."

"Thanks," was all Tina could say as she darted down the hall.

Hank was not as spry as he once was, and Tina outdistanced him. Hank finally reached the waiting room to find Tina nose to nose with Roy. Everybody in the waiting area was watching.

The waiting area was about thirty feet square with four rows of cushioned chairs facing a big screen TV. Tina and Roy were in the far corner when Hank walked in.

"How could you let that little boy ride a range ram when Miguel had already told you he was mean?" Tina hissed.

"We had the dogs ready, and Josh wanted to try, so I let him," Roy responded in an exasperated voice. He continued, "I love that boy like he's my own. I would never do anything that I thought would hurt him. Can't you understand that?"

"What I understand is that you are the most irresponsible person I've ever met. You never ask what I want, and you don't listen to me when I tell you."

"This isn't about you, Tina; it's about Josh. All I hear you say is what *you* want. Get a grip," Roy said in a stern voice.

A voice from the side doors had Hank, Tina, and Roy all turning to see who had spoken.

"If that young man hadn't been wearing that helmet and hadn't had his mouthpiece in, he would be dead," the man dressed in green said. "That, young lady, you can take to the bank."

Tina almost collapsed when the doctor said the word "dead." Roy caught her with his arms, and he still held her as the doctor finished. Hank sat down and was shaking his head back and forth.

"Your boy had a terrible accident. One unforeseen and I think unintentional. That helmet saved his life. He has a concussion, a broken right arm, and when he comes to, he will have one hell of a headache. As it stands right now, he will be in ICU until he regains consciousness, and then we'll see. We operated to relieve pressure from the brain, and we will monitor him until we're sure everything is stable. It will probably take a few days. You can visit him later tonight, but plan on him being here for maybe a week."

"Now, young lady, if this young man had not acted responsibly and not had the wherewithal to call the helicopter, we might be having a different discussion. This was an accident, with no blame."

The doctor stood, "I'll see you later with an update. As for now, I suggest you find a motel because you're going to be here a while." He shook hands with Roy and left.

Tina turned into Roy's shoulder and sobbed quietly. Roy wrapped his arm around her shoulders and held her. Hank stood and held them both.

*  *  *  *  *  *  *

The Malibu jumped to life when Maggie turned the key. Preacher had always liked the way the old muscle cars sounded. He swung into the bucket seat of the passenger side. The dash was black. The console was black with chrome trim. As Preacher settled in, he noticed that the black carpet complemented the remaining white interior. Preacher was impressed.

Maggie pulled the T-handle back into reverse. "Wanna go for a ride?" she asked.

"Lead the way," Preacher said as he buckled up his seat belt.

Maggie backed away from the station. "Hang on," she said. Squealing tires was all that could be heard when Maggie pulled it back into drive and stood on the accelerator.

It made Preacher smile to watch the excitement take over her body. Her shorts were shorter, her foot was on the floor, and she was leaning into the steering wheel.

Preacher had had his share of party girls in his life. They were fun, for awhile. This was a side of Maggie he hadn't counted on. What the hell, he thought, I'm only going to be here a few days; might as well enjoy it. It surprised him when she took her foot off the accelerator and settled back in her seat.

"I've been wanting to do that for a long time—thanks, Preacher."

"Why thank me; I'm only here for the ride."

"You rattled me back at the station. It's been a long time since I've felt like letting go. I may not be twenty-five anymore, but it does feel good to be wanted. Driving my car is a good release. Thanks, Preacher, for making me feel that way. I needed it," she said in a relieved voice.

Preacher smiled, "So, where is this place you're taking me?" Preacher was relieved that Maggie wasn't a partier. He had had enough of that life. His concern now was what to do with the rest of his life. A full-time party did not fit into that scenario.

"It's a little spot I discovered when I was a young girl. It's pretty, and it's secluded. I go there at times to think, and I go there to take in some sun, in private."

"So...you're taking me to a place where we can go skinny dippin'?"

She smiled and looked over at Preacher, "Yup, but I wouldn't suggest it tonight. You won't get dry before you get cold. We don't want you sick. I'm not done with you yet."

"Okay...and just what do you have in mind?" he asked.

"Hang on and find out," she said as she took the green car up to ninety miles per hour. The gravel road that Maggie took from the highway looked like a forest service road. The few trees were scrubs, and there was a lot of sage and rabbit brush. The road curved to the left after about a quarter of a mile then back to the right. As they turned back to the right, Preacher noticed that the scrub trees formed a barrier between them and the road. It only took a few minutes for Maggie to come to another side road and head back east. Within a mile, Maggie came to a stand of willows that was surrounded by green grass. A small pond glistened with the evening sun. A huge flat rock sat majestically half in and half out of the water. It was there that Maggie led him.

"Well, what do you think of my little hidey-hole?" she asked.

"Looks like a spot to get comfortable, as long as you don't get any intruders," Preacher said as he sat down on the rock, stretched out his legs, and leaned back on his hands.

"Most people know this place is here, and a few use it. Usually, I have it all to myself," Maggie said. "This is where I come when I've had enough of life and want to take a break. It's quiet. A person can forget all the annoyances for awhile." She paused and sat next to Preacher, crossed her legs and put her hands in her lap. "I was thinking that if you were still here come Sunday, we might have a picnic out here. It's been a long time since I've had a picnic."

"Maggie," Preacher said in a warning voice, "I may not be here Sunday. I'm leaving as soon as Hank and that little boy come home."

"I know," she replied dejectedly, "but if you're still here, it would be fun, wouldn't it?"

"I think anything we did would be fun. If I'm still here, we'll come out here for your picnic. I hear you make some damn good fried chicken, and I've already tried your potato salad. So, if it works out, you have a date."

"You make me feel good, Preacher. Better than I have for a while."

"I could make you feel a lot better, you know."

"Braggart," she said as she stood up in one fluid motion and jumped off the rock.

"No brag, just fact," Preacher said with a smile.

"Well, right now, I would feel better if we went back so I could check on my mother and fix you something to eat. I did say I would feed ya, besides, it'll be dark soon. Come on, Romeo, let's go," she said as she sashayed toward the car.

Preacher remembered the last time he had watched her walk away from him, definitely eye candy.

When Maggie pulled up to the bay doors of the station it was indeed getting dark. "If you'll move your bike, I'll pull this beauty in so it'll be here for you in the morning," she said.

"We can do that," Preacher responded.

Preacher got out and brushed his hand over the fender of the green machine as he walked up to the door.

* * * * * * *

When Tina had relaxed a little, she withdrew from Roy and looked up at him. "I'm sorry, Roy, for yelling at you. I'm just so scared. If anything were to happen to that little boy, I don't know if I could deal with it."

"I know," replied Roy. "Don't worry, we'll get through this. I promise. I won't leave you until we can all go home, together."

"Thank you," she said as she laid her head back on his chest.

"Hank," Roy continued, "I'll go find us a place to stay and be back as soon as I can."

"That's fine, son," Hank said. "I'll stay here with Tina until you get back."

"You're not going to stay?" Roy asked.

"It's been a long day, and I'm tired. I'm not going anywhere tonight. I'll call Preacher and see if he'll stay for a couple of days until we can get Josh released."

"If you want, I'll call," Roy said.

"No," Hank replied, "I have to talk to Maggie as well. Find us a room, and we'll go from there. You might want to call your dad, though, and tell him what's going on."

"Okay," Roy said. He kissed Tina's head and said, "I'll see ya soon."

"Thanks," Tina said.

"Roy," Hank said, "try to find a cheaper motel, like *Super 8* or something; I don't think we'll be spending a lot of time there, and we need to think about our expenses. This is not going to be a cheap visit."

With a nod of his head, Roy left to find a room.

* * * * * * *

Maggie had gone home after putting the Malibu in Hank's first bay for Preacher. She was now standing in the bedroom, thinking about what might have happened if she had let Preacher take control in the station earlier. She felt the tingle as it started in her stomach and worked its way down to her center. It was going to be impossible to control her body if she didn't do something. Preacher had acted like the perfect gentleman for the afternoon, and that had Maggie thinking. She had wanted to be touched. She had wanted him to touch her. Now, here she was, standing half naked in her bedroom, wanting him all over her. She had to do something.

To take her mind off Preacher, she turned to what she did best: cook. She pulled a pizza out of the freezer and turned on the oven. Cheese, onions, and olives came out next. With little effort, she grated the cheese, sliced olives, and chopped onions.

She piled them all on the frozen pizza and popped it in the oven. With the pizza in the oven, she now returned to her bedroom. She pulled out a pair of jeans and replaced the shorts she had on. What a hussy, she thought as she looked at the small amount of material it took to make up the shorts. She had Levi cut-offs, but had opted for these for the way they enhanced her waist and made her legs look longer. She had dressed for him.

A woman could have an itch the same as a man. Maggie had always gone to town when this mood struck her. Small towns know everything. Even if you're discreet, they still seem to know. What would Tina think if she knew what Maggie was thinking? She would tease her unmercifully.

Maggie knew Preacher would have taken her if she had let him, but something had stopped her. She wanted to be part of his history, not just a quickie. That part had stopped her. His casual way of referring to sex had told her he was interested, but he had acted like the perfect gentleman, not even another attempt for a kiss. Nothing.

The timer on the oven brought her out of her dream world. The pizza was done. Putting her moccasins back on, she walked back into the kitchen to retrieve their dinner.

Preacher had opted for a shower after Maggie had gone home to check on her mother and make dinner. Surprisingly, the hot water was almost instant when he turned on the faucet. After the shower, Preacher washed out his socks and shorts and now hung them in his room on a coat hanger. He put his Levi's back on, as well as clean socks and his boots. He heard the back door open and looked out of his room to see who it might be, when Maggie called out his name.

"Preacher, are you here?"

"Hello, Maggie," Preacher said as he went back to his laundry.

"Are you hungry?" she asked.

"And what would you be talking about, food or another hunger?"

Maggie flushed. Her being a redhead, the crimson of her face and neck glowed.

"Pizza, that's what I'm talking about. I added a few things to the topping, and I brought over a couple of beers for you. You like pizza?"

"Have you ever known a biker that didn't like pizza?" he asked.

"No, I don't think I ever have."

She had changed from the shorts to Levi's but still wore the sassy little top and her moccasins.

"You'll not find one here either," Preacher replied.

Maggie could only stare at the scars and tattoos. His chest was broad, and his hips were narrow. She felt the tingle again.

"We should maybe eat in the office, don't you think?" Maggie offered.

"Wherever you choose," Preacher said as he pulled on another T-shirt.

"We don't want to be the town gossip, you know," Maggie stated. "If the neighbors can't see us, tongues will start waggin'. We can't have that. You have a reputation to uphold."

"My virtue is the last thing these people will want to talk about, but it might damage yours," Preacher said.

"My reputation has been hashed out in this town for so many years; I don't think anybody cares anymore."

"Well then, let's eat out in the office and give them something not to talk about."

"Preacher, as I said earlier, you're history already in this town. I don't think you could do anything that the whole community wouldn't talk about."

"Let them talk. I'm not going to be here long, and I don't think I'll be back, so let them talk. You have to live here," Preacher said.

"Okay, pizza in the office," she replied.

They only ate half of the pizza. Neither Preacher nor Maggie drank the beer. When Maggie asked if he wanted one, he politely refused.

"I think I'll wander out to the tree for awhile. Care to join me?" Preacher asked.

"Only if I can wear your jacket; it's cold out there," she said as she wiped off the desk and closed the pizza box.

"Yeah, I noticed that your headlights are on," he said.

Maggie blushed.

The ringing phone broke the mood. Maggie looked at Preacher, who motioned with his hand for Maggie to answer.

"Hello...yes, it's Maggie, Hank. How's Josh?"

Preacher didn't feel the need to talk right now. Maggie sat back down and was listening intently. Preacher was ready for his night cap. After he rolled his evening doobie, he strolled out to the tree.

Preacher looked back at the station when he heard the front door open. Maggie was a silhouette against the lights of the office. Her snug Levi's, Preacher's leather jacket, and her hair brushed out made her look like a survivor walking away from a catastrophe in a movie.

Damn, that's one hell of a woman, Preacher thought. As Maggie drew closer, Preacher asked, "What's the verdict?"

"Josh is hurt bad, Preacher. He has a concussion and a broken arm. He's still in ICU until he's stable. Preacher, he hasn't regained consciousness. This could be bad," she said as she sat down next to him.

"He'll make it. I feel it. That's one tough little boy," Preacher replied.

"Well, that's the bad news; now for the good news."

"And, just what would that be?" Preacher asked.

"The doctor said that Josh will have to stay in the hospital a while until they're sure there isn't any more fluid on the brain."

"And that's the good news?"

"Yes, now I get my picnic."

"Great," was all Preacher said.

* * * * * * *

Roy returned an hour later. He had asked at the information center if there were any motels in the area and had been given a list of the ones that gave a discount to the family members of the patients. He went to two before he found a vacancy. He took one that had two queen beds and a small kitchenette.

Hank was dozing when Roy returned. Roy checked with information upon his return and was told that Josh was out of recovery and had been moved to ICU.

"Hank," Roy called softly, "Hank, I'm back."

Hank came awake with a start. "What happened?" he asked as his eyes focused.

"Hank, I'm back. I took us a room down the road about half a mile—two beds and a kitchen. I thought Tina would probably stay here, at least until Josh wakes up. The kitchen will save us money too."

"Good," Hank replied.

Roy sat beside Hank. "How's Tina holding up?" Roy asked.

"About as good as can be expected," Hank replied.

"And Josh?"

"He's not awake, but the doctor is optimistic. He said sometimes the brain won't wake up for a day or so after such a trauma."

Roy said, "When his head hit that fence it sounded like you dropped a melon on concrete. I've never been so scared in my life. When I got to him and he was just lying there, I thought I'd lost him."

Hank put a comforting hand on Roy's leg, "Let's thank God you didn't; Tina would've killed you."

Roy chuckled, "Yeah...she would have."

"Maybe something good will come out of this if we give it a chance."

"You think?" Roy asked.

"Well, you saved her son's life. I think she'll remember that." Hank stood up and looked down at Roy, "Come on," he said, "let's go see Tina."

* * * * * * *

"What, don't you want to take me on a picnic?" Maggie asked.

"That's not what I said."

"Well, then why did you say 'great' like that? I think a picnic would be fun."

"Maggie, I'm not here to have fun. I left on this journey to get my head on straight, not babysit an old man."

Maggie turned toward him. "What are you running away from, Preacher?"

"I'm not running away from anything. I'm hopefully riding toward something."

"And, what would that be?" she asked.

"I don't know," Preacher said as he looked up at the stars. "I guess I'll know when I get there."

"I hope you find what you're looking for, Preacher."

"That's why I'm here, Maggie; that's why I'm here."

"Good night, Preacher," Maggie said as she stood and looked down at Preacher. "See ya for breakfast?" she asked.

"With cold pizza in the fridge, that's the breakfast of champions. It don't get no better than that," Preacher declared.

Maggie chuckled. "Okay; I'll bring your jacket back later?"

"Sure."

"You are a hard one, Preacher."

"I'll show you a hard one," he responded.

"I'll just bet you could," she said in a playful voice.

Maggie leaned down and pulled his head up. She looked deep into his eyes and brushed her lips across his. "Good night, Preacher."

"See ya later," he responded.

* * * * * * *

Maggie's night shirt was an oversized T-shirt with a Budweiser logo. She had left Preacher by the tree, smoking. Now, she was lying in her bed, wide awake, thinking about him. You've got it bad, girl, she was thinking. You've only known him two days, and you're having carnal thoughts about him. Maggie tried to go to sleep, but the tingle had now turned into a throb.

I could always touch myself, she thought, or use my toy in the night stand, but that just wouldn't be the same. I want to be with him. I want him to touch me. I want him to take me to Heaven. I want him, damn it. The floor was cold as she swung her feet off the bed and planted them solidly on the cold surface. She slipped on her moccasins and stood. You'd better go now, Maggie, she told herself, before you lose your nerve. She grabbed Preacher's jacket, put it on over her T-shirt, and headed out the door.

Preacher heard a strange sound. He reached into his saddle bags. His hand came out with a .38 Special. He slipped out the door barefoot and faded into the darkness. When the back door opened, Preacher was standing beside it. All Maggie heard was the audible click as Preacher pulled back the hammer.

"Preacher, is that you?"

"Who did you expect? Hank?" Preacher said from behind her.

"You scared me. Nobody has ever pulled a gun on me before."

"Keep sneaking around, and the next time it could get you shot," Preacher said as he returned to his room and turned on the light.

"I didn't come here to rob you."

"I can see that by your attire."

"Well, I couldn't sleep so I came over to see if you wanted some company."

"A man can always use a woman's company. Just what was it you wanted?"

Maggie stared at him for a moment. Then walked over to the bed, took off Preacher's jacket, pulled the sleeping bag open, sat, and swung her legs in. "Why don't I just show you," she said as she patted the bed.

Preacher slid off his Levi's and crawled in beside her. "Okay, show me," he said.

She slid up close, swung her leg over his to straddle him. "I *will* see starbursts, Preacher," she said as she lowered herself onto him.

"I'll do my best," he said. She leaned forward for a kiss she hoped would last until morning. It did. They were both too involved to notice the symphony the bed was playing.

* * * * * * *

Hank and Roy found Tina in Josh's room. She was curled up in a huge overstuffed chair that looked as if it was trying to absorb her. Roy was amazed at the number of machines that were attached to his little boy. Josh looked small in the hospital bed. His head had been shaved and was now wrapped in gauze and white tape. His eyes were black. Where they had attached all the tubes and wires he could only imagine. He looked like a puppet awaiting the puppeteer. The cast was a bright white on his right arm.

He's definitely going to have a headache, Roy thought.

"Tina," Hank called in a soft voice, "are you awake?"

"Yes," she said in a small voice.

Roy looked over at her as she uncoiled from within the chair's grasp. She was still in her waitress uniform. The slacks were wrinkled, and the blouse was smudged with her makeup and tears. Her face was drawn. She was exhausted. Today had been a hard one.

"How's our little man?" Roy asked as he moved to stand beside her and put his hand gently on her shoulder.

"I don't know. The doctor hasn't been back. He looks so small and fragile lying there," she said as she looked at the boy and placed her hand upon Roy's.

"Have they said anything?" Hank asked.

"The nurse said he is stable, but he won't wake up. She said they won't release him to the wards until he does. She said the same thing the doctor said, "Sometimes it takes a day or two."

"He'll be okay," Hank said.

"I hope so, Daddy," she replied in a tired voice.

"Well, one thing's for sure," Roy stated, "he ain't gonna win the mutton bustin' at the rodeo."

"Isn't," Tina corrected with a smile.

"Isn't," countered Roy.

"Tina, Roy got us a room down the street a ways, so we have some place to stay. It has a kitchenette, so we can cook, and only two beds, so one of us can stay here with Josh until we go home," Hank said matter-of-factly.

"I'm not leaving until I'm sure he's okay, Dad." The way Tina said it, there was no doubt.

"Hank," Roy said, "you look dead on your feet. Why don't you go back to the motel and get some sleep. I'll stay here with Tina."

"I am sorta tired," Hank said; "maybe I will. Come and get me if anything changes, will ya?"

"Not to worry, Hank, I'll come and get you if anything changes," Roy replied.

"Honey, are you going to be okay?" Hank asked.

"I'll be okay. I just can't have Josh waking up and me not be here. He'll be confused and scared."

"I know; I know. Just settle down and relax,Tina, everything is going to be okay."

"I hope so," Tina replied. "I don't know what I'd do if it wasn't. We'll just trust in God."

"Now go get some sleep, Dad," she continued, "Roy can stay here with me." She looked up at Roy, "That is if he wants to."

"He wants to," Roy replied.

"Good; I'll be back after I'm rested."

"Goodnight, Hank," Roy said.

"Goodnight, Roy," Hank replied as he headed for the door.

"Did anyone call Maggie and give her an update?" Tina asked.

"Yes, we called. Everyone is concerned and sends their best wishes."

"I'm glad you stayed, Roy. I don't know if I could get through this without you and Dad here. He's all I've got," she said as the tears rolled down her cheeks. "I need a hug," she said.

"Me too," Roy said as he embraced her.

* * * * * * *

When Preacher awoke, the only light was the moon, illuminating through the bay doors. The warmth from Maggie's body had the sleeping bag as warm as a cocoon. Maggie had thrown her leg over his, and her arm circled his chest. Her head rested on his shoulder. The night had been an adventure for both of them. He didn't know what time they had drifted off to sleep, but it hadn't been all that long ago. She stirred, but didn't wake. Preacher ran his hand over her bare leg, remembering the gymnastics they had gone through. Maybe it wouldn't be so bad to stay around for a day or two. She was an energetic lover. She was a woman who knew what she wanted and how to get it from her man. He smiled. He felt her stir.

"I see you're happy to see me this morning," she said as she rose up on an elbow.

"I think you broke something last night," Preacher said.

"Too bad," she said with a smile.

"I haven't felt this good in ages," she purred. "So, buck up, Preacher. As long as you're here, I'm going to use you. I'll cook for you; I'll do your laundry, and I'll sleep with you. How's that for a deal?"

"I can deal with that," he said.

"What about this poor old bed?" he continued; "I don't think it can take much more abuse."

"Not to worry. Tomorrow we'll sleep in my bed, and the next day is our picnic."

"Your mind is set on that picnic isn't it?"

"Yes," she stated matter-of-factly; "yes, it is." Then she rolled over to straddle him again.

"It's pretty out there, and I haven't been on a date in years. I don't socialize with the single population around here because of the diner. The last thing I need is some man mooching off me—been there, done that. With you here helping Hank, and me helping Tina, people will expect us to be together. Sooo...let's be together. As long as we're somewhat discreet, people will accept that. They may speculate some, but so what. It'll be fun, Preacher, out by the pond, on that rock," she said with a wiggle and a smile.

She was looking down at Preacher. He couldn't make out the facial features, but with her hair down, the image was that of a goddess. "This is inconvenient for both of us," she said; "I'm out a waitress, and you're delayed on your adventure. Let's make the best of it. Let's have some fun. When you leave, it'll go back to the same old thing. I want to have memories, Preacher. I want you to be a part of my history. Can you understand that?"

He hesitated. "What time do you have to be at the diner?" he asked.

"Around five o'clock. That way I can make the biscuits and put on the coffee. This being Saturday, it's going to be busy," she replied as she settled on him. "That's only about two hours from now. Let's make some memories."

"You silver tongued devil, now you're talking my language."

* * * * * * *

Preacher stood at the back door as he had yesterday, coffee cup in hand. Maggie had left before daylight. She had told him she had to shower, change, and check on her mother before she started with the diner. She had been gone about an hour. He glanced over at the ravine and noticed the rabbit he had seen yesterday morning. Looking over at the green expanse inside the white fence, Preacher saw that the rest of them were on the lawn. He saluted them with his coffee cup. This is a quiet place, he thought. He could understand why Hank had settled here. Preacher preferred the tall fir trees of northern California, but the desert had its own mystique.

Preacher retraced his steps back into the bay. The Malibu awaited him. He found the electrical panel and looked for the breakers for the gas pumps. They were still on, but he made a mental note to shut them off at closing time. He opened the bay doors and headed for his room to get a piece of pizza. Maggie had put it in the little fridge. Grabbing a slice, he headed out front.

The lights were on in the diner. Maggie looked busy as she scampered in front of the windows. This is going to be as hard on her as it's going to be for me, Preacher thought. She will have to cook and waitress. I'll bet she won't be as active tonight as she was last night. The thought made him chuckle. He surveyed the second bay. She had her work, and he had his. He might as well get started.

Hank had told him that he didn't open until eight, but Hank wasn't here. The extra hour or so might generate a few extra dollars for the coffers. Hank and Tina were going to need it.

Preacher remembered how much the medical bills had been when his daughter was in the hospital. She had been diagnosed with cancer. It took a year for the disease to take her young life. The bills had been astronomical. This could break Hank. With that thought in mind, Preacher started looking. He wanted a coffee can or something. Unable to find what he was looking for at the station, he headed for *Maggie's*. The door was open, and the smells coming from the kitchen were tantalizing.

"Maggie," he called as he walked in.

"Back here, Preacher," she called from the kitchen. Maggie had her hands in a round pile of dough. "Grab a cup of coffee and take a load off," she said as Preacher strolled into the kitchen.

The kitchen was not as big as Preacher had first thought. A service counter about six feet long was under the service window where the food was passed out to the counter. A large black grill was to its left with an oven under it. The center of the room was occupied by a large chopping block prep table. A glistening chandelier of pots and pans hung over the table. The back wall was covered in stainless steel. Big stainless steel sinks filled most of the space with what looked like a sanitizer toward the front of the building. That area was filled with refrigerators and upright freezers. Maggie had her hair up in her standard bun on top of her head and was in her uniform.

"Biscuits and gravy?" Preacher asked as he pointed at the large pile of dough.

"Yup, you'll have to wait to get some; the biscuits aren't ready."

"I'm not here to get some; I'm still trying to recover from last night," Preacher said with a smirk.

"Well then, what do you want?" she asked with a smile.

"I need a coffee can or something. Do you have a can or a jar that I can use?"

Maggie stopped kneading the dough. "What on earth do you need a coffee can for?"

"Well, I thought we could put it out on the counter and ask for donations; anything to help Hank and Tina. Everybody knows what happened, and I thought they might want to help," Preacher responded.

"Look under the service counter. I think you might find something in there. No, wait," she suddenly said, "I have an empty gallon jar in my apartment. Give me a minute, and I'll get it for you."

Preacher leaned against the counter. Watching Maggie knead the dough, Preacher understood how she stayed in shape.

"You make biscuits every morning?" he asked.

"Every morning except Sunday," she replied as she attacked the mound of dough.

"The gravy homemade as well?"

"No, I buy the canned stuff then doctor it up. It's really pretty good."

She patted the dough ball flat and reached for a rolling pin. It took all her weight leaning on the rolling pin, but she rolled it out to about one half an inch thick. After grabbing two large baking sheets, she began to cut out biscuits.

"You're a regular Julia Childs aren't you?" Preacher commented.

Maggie looked over at him and smiled. "No, but I do know what the men around here want for breakfast: meat and eggs, fried, with biscuits and gravy. Saturdays are always busy."

Maggie finished cutting the biscuits and laid them out on trays. "We'll let them rise for a minute while I go and get that jar."

Maggie came back with a glass gallon jar that said mayonnaise on the label. "Will this work?"

"That will work just fine," Preached replied. "All I need now is a piece of paper and a pen. I think Hank has that over at the station."

Maggie put the jar on the counter and wrapped her arms around his neck. "You're a good man, Preacher, to think about Josh and want to help."

Preacher put his hands around her hips. "We all need help from time to time, and hospital visits aren't cheap. I'd bet Hank has helped most of these old boys around here at one time or another. Now it's time to help him."

She leaned up and gave him a tender kiss, "You taste like pizza. Was that your breakfast?"

"Breakfast of champions," he said with a smile as he gave her backside a gentle pat. "See you later, Maggie."

As he turned to leave, Maggie swatted his butt and smiled. "See you later, Preacher."

* * * * * * *

Hank awoke at five-thirty disoriented. He had been exhausted when he arrived at the motel. The room Roy had rented was small. Two queen size beds, a dresser, one nightstand, and a chair with a small round table comprised the furnishings. The kitchenette had a small counter with a sink, a microwave, and a hot plate. A small coffee pot was sitting on the hot plate. The ornate mirror over the dresser was as old as the print that decorated the opposite wall. Hank looked in the mirror and shook his head. He needed a shave. I need to find a store around here, he thought. Finding a writing tablet in the nightstand, along with a Bible, he began to compose a list.

They had left in a hurry. Nobody cared about the amenities necessary for the stay. They hadn't even thought; they just left.

Shower first; shopping second. Hank stepped into the shower.

* * * * * * *

Hank arrived at the hospital all showered and shaved. He checked with the front desk and was informed that Josh was still in ICU with no change.

Hank found Roy in the waiting area, asleep. He knew Tina would not leave Josh until he came to. He found her curled up in the overstuffed chair, asleep. These kids will stay together for Josh, Hank thought. I just hope they're smart enough to stay together after that. Hank picked what looked like a comfortable chair and sat down to wait.

* * * * * * *

The diner was indeed busy. Not only was it Saturday, but the customers had a central topic for discussion: the accident. The donation jar that Preacher had conveniently placed next to the cash register caught almost all the change, and the twenty that he called seed money, gathered other greenbacks at a continual pace. Everybody wanted an updated report and then offered their opinion.

Preacher placed second as the other topic of conversation. How could Hank trust a biker, an outsider, to watch the station? Who keeps track of the money? Where is he staying? Aren't you afraid, with an outlaw across the street?

Maggie did her best to downplay Preacher but found herself defending him.

Gene, Roy's father, came in around eight.

"Good morning, Gene," Maggie said as she poured his coffee. "Have you heard from Roy this morning?"

"No, not since last night," he replied.

"Have you heard anything?" he asked.

"No; Hank called last night, but I haven't heard anything this morning," she replied.

"The boys at the ranch want to help but didn't know what they could do. Miguel feels the worst. He feels responsible." Gene continued, "How's the Preacher doing over at the station?"

"Gene, he's working most of the time. He asked me to take care of the money for Hank. He doesn't want to be responsible. Last night he gave me everything except thirty dollars and some change for the till. If you want to help, Preacher set up this jar for donations. Hank and Tina are going to need it. I hate to think about how much this is going to cost, but anything will help. Tell Miguel to pass the hat if he wants to."

"I'll tell him," Gene concluded.

"What are ya havin' for breakfast?" she asked.

"Biscuits and gravy," he responded.

Maggie turned toward the kitchen but couldn't help wonder how much this was going to cost the whole community.

* * * * * * *

Preacher set the hoist under the Malibu and lifted the beauty up. He walked under it to survey the undercarriage. Whoever built this classic had sprayed undercoat not only in the wheel wells, but the whole undercarriage was dimpled.

A grease gun hung from the ceiling. As long as I'm here, Preacher thought. He grabbed the gun, pulled down some hose, and started with the U-joints. He checked the rear end and found it full. He lowered it down and started taking off tires. Preacher liked working on these older cars. Everything was simple. Finding Hank's brake tools was another story. He found them in a drawer in one of the tool boxes. He backed off the adjusters and pulled the drums. The drums weren't scarred, so a little emery cloth for the shine, and they were done. He was taking off the front brakes when Gene sauntered in.

"How's it going?" he asked.

"Fine," Preacher responded and went back to the brakes.

"Maggie brought this car home with her a couple of years ago; doesn't drive it much. She takes her mom's truck when she goes to town."

Preacher knew Gene had something on his mind, so he opted for silence.

"How you holding out?" Gene asked.

"Fine," Preacher responded again.

"Preacher, if there's anything we can do for Hank, let us know, and we'll try to help," he said.

"Maggie's the boss of that department, but if you want to help me, those tires need to be fixed," Preacher said, gesturing toward the row of tires.

Gene chuckled, "I didn't mean fixin' tires."

"Well, anything you can do to help Hank make money is the best help. He's going to need it."

"That he is," Gene said.

"Other than the money, maybe you could have one of your boys come in and mow Hank's lawn or something." Preacher had seen this kind of help before: all talk, no action. "Maybe you should talk to Maggie. She seems to run the show around here."

"That she does," Gene said as he walked out to the tree.

Preacher had to smile at the old boys already gathering around the tree. They will watch me until Hank comes home, he thought. Let's give them something to think about. Preacher attacked the brakes with a vengeance.

The brakes on Maggie's car were not that bad but were getting close to the rivets. Preacher had worked in a gas station as a teenager. Changing brakes was something he could do and not really think about it. He found himself thinking about his own little girl. All the money in the world would not have saved her from the aggressive cancer. His wife had blamed him for her illness. Preacher's father had died from cancer. She insisted that the little girl had inherited the deadly disease. A sticky divorce had started the dominos falling, ending in a bankruptcy.

Preacher had walked out of the courtroom broke and alone. The irony of the super lotto made him smile. He had one dollar in his pocket when he walked out of the courtroom that day. In a reckless gesture, he had bought one ticket for the Saturday night drawing. It had netted him millions. Now, he had more money than he could spend and nobody to share it with.

That's why you're here, he thought, to figure out what you have to do to get some happiness back into your life. Money isn't everything.

Preacher cleaned the mags prior to replacing them on the big green machine. He lowered the classic to the floor. After finding a hose, which was not an easy task, he started to wash Maggie's car.

* * * * * * *

Gene had been watching Preacher as he worked. He was a man that had grown up with hard work. He appreciated the style that the biker used while working: clean and efficient. The gas customers were treated with respect. He washed every windshield, always said thank you and have a good day. The apprehension he had felt began to diminish. He had even gone so far as to tell the boys around the tree, "Well, gentlemen, I don't think we have to worry about Hank's station. It looks like that Preacher has it under control."

* * * * * * *

The traffic at *Maggie's* had slowed down when Preacher walked over to the diner. Maggie was busing tables and pouring coffee for the few customers that remained when he walked in.

"Be right with ya, Preacher," she said when she looked up and noticed him.

Preacher nodded his acknowledgement as he walked over to the counter. The jar was half full of bills, with change covering the bottom.

"It looks like people are willing to help Josh," he said when Maggie came back to the counter with the dirty dishes.

"That's all I've done this morning, is answer questions about the accident. How's it going over at the station? I noticed you washing my baby, thank you."

"Your brakes were the only thing on the agenda this morning; they're done. Where do want me to park it?"

"There's a garage behind the diner. The key is on the ring. If you have time, please put it in there," she said as she set the dishes aside.

"That works," he replied.

"Did you want something, Preacher?"

"I'm still tired from last night, but I will take a biscuit with a piece of sausage in the middle, if you're offering."

Maggie shook her head, set the coffee pot on the prep table and split a biscuit. She handed the sandwich to him and said in a laughing voice, "Now, get out of here before we embarrass my customers. Are you going to want lunch?"

"No, I think this will hold me," he said holding the biscuit up to survey it. She had stuck in a thick patty of meat that stuck out the edges. Preacher was eating the sandwich as he walked back to the station.

When Preacher returned from delivering Maggie's car, he pushed his bike out into the sunshine. The entire shop was a mess. The first bay from brake dust, the second from lack of attention. He was going to give it his attention.

He found a barrel dolly out back, some solvent in a barrel, and another box of borax in a cabinet. He took the barrels, one empty and one with solvent in it out back and put them up on pallets. The tires in front of the tire machine he stacked outside between the two bays. He emptied the tube tank and took it out front. He kept at it until the floors of both bays were bare.

The workbench across the back wall was a different story. Most of the treasures he found on the bench were garbage. The dirty rags went into a bag to be laundered. All the tools that had been scattered from one end of the bench to the other were wiped off and put back in the tool boxes. Those tool boxes will have to wait for another day, he thought as he put the tools away. He did find a coffee can, and he put some solvent in it. Using a semi-clean rag, he wiped down the metal surface of the bench as well as the cabinet doors.

Maggie walked over about ten o'clock; she was smiling. "The boys were wondering when you're going to paint."

"Right after I get this place mucked out."

"I told them that if they had the paint, they could do it tomorrow, before breakfast," she said with a chuckle. "You've impressed them, Preacher."

"Yeah, well, impressed or not, I'm not painting. I hate to paint."

Looking around at the bare station, Maggie asked, "Just what are you doing?"

"Like I said, I'm cleaning this mess up. You know, 'everything has its place'".

"Hank won't be able to find anything when he gets back."

"Too bad. He leaves me here to watch this place; he should expect me to do something. All I've done is Gene's exhaust system and your brakes. When I get through with cleaning, I'll fix those flats. That ought to make him some money. I have a hard time doing nothing. I'm getting bored. Cleaning up this place gives me something to do."

Maggie smiled, "Then get back to cleaning. I don't want you bored." As she started to walk back to the diner, she stopped and turned around, "Do you want anything now?" she asked.

"What are you offering?"

"Not what you're thinking, at least not yet. I was thinking about a cold drink or something."

"A glass of that tea you had yesterday would be good, if that's all you're offering."

"You got it," she replied as she turned back toward the diner.

Preacher watched her walk back across the street. Not even a panty line, he thought. She didn't have any on last night, but that was to be expected. He wondered if she was wearing them now. Smiling, Preacher went back to work.

* * * * * * *

The doctor arrived at ten-thirty. He found Hank in the waiting room watching TV. "Good morning, Mr. Kyle. I'm Doctor Nixon. I operated on your grandson yesterday."

Hank stood and offered his hand, "I remember your speech. You didn't mince any words yesterday, so please, don't now. How's my grandson doing?" Hank stuck his hands in his pockets.

"Well," the doctor started, "I don't know. I haven't seen the charts yet, but I think that the boy will wake up today. What do you say to having a look, and then we can all sit down, and I'll tell you what to expect?"

"Lead the way, Doc."

Tina and Roy were sitting side by side watching TV, with no sound. *Mute* was displayed at the bottom of the screen. Both of them looked exhausted. They hadn't left Josh or each other alone since the ordeal began. The doctor had stopped at the nurse's station to look at the charts.

"Roy, Tina, the doctor's here," Hank said.

"Where is he?" they asked quietly in unison.

"He's out at the nurse's station. He said he wanted to check with them before he talks to us."

"Good morning," the doctor said as he entered the small room. "How's our patient?"

"He hasn't woken up yet; is he going to be okay?" Tina asked. She was squeezing Roy's hand so hard it had gone white.

"I think so. His heart rate is back up to normal, and his respiratory rate has increased; that's a good sign. That means his body is getting ready. Why don't we go out to the waiting area so we can talk?"

They entered the waiting room before the doctor who had stopped at the nurse's station again. He arrived a short time after the family. He wasn't wearing the green hospital pants and shirt. His slacks and shirt were pressed. Hank put his hands in his pockets. Tina and Roy sat.

"Okay, folks, here's what's happening. Josh's body wants to wake up. His brain is still undecided. From looking at the charts, I would think that sometime today, he will wake up. His vision may be fuzzy, and his throat will be dry from the oxygen. He will have a headache. We have him on a small amount of pain medicine, so it shouldn't be bad. Don't let him get excited. Let him wake up on his own. If you notice any movement, alert the nurses. I've told them what I want, and they will do it. He's not out of the woods yet, but if all goes well, we should move him to a ward tomorrow. Ms. Kyle, I suggest you get some rest."

"I'm not leaving until my boy wakes up and I know he'll be okay," Tina said in her all too familiar aggressive voice.

"Okay, okay," the doctor conceded; "suit yourself. I've asked the nurses to page me when he wakes up, so I'll see you then."

"Thank you," Tina and Roy said.

* * * * * * *

Preacher was still smiling at the image of Maggie walking back to the diner as he sloshed some solvent on the heavy grease spots. I might need a scraper in that second bay, he thought. He found a stiff-bristled shop broom behind the back door. He swept out the office first, next was his bedroom. Now he could get the solvent smeared around, add a little water, sprinkle some soap over the entire floor, and let it sit awhile.

The gas customers had slowed down after the morning rush, so Preacher had some time. He changed the water in the windshield squeegee tank and added more paper towels. Next, he emptied the barrel of trash from the pumps. Now it's time to clean the floor. Grabbing the shop broom, he began scrubbing the bays. The first bay came clean with little effort. The second, however, was more of a challenge. Preacher had to use a shovel on some of the spots—the ones behind the tire tank and compressor. It only took an hour. He was rinsing the floor when Gene wandered in.

"Preacher, Hank won't know this place when he comes back. I don't think I've ever seen it so clean."

"I've got nothing better to do except leave, but I promised Hank I'd stay. So...here I am."

"Yeah, well, I've talked with the boys, and we would like to give you some business."

"Okay," Preacher replied, "what do you have in mind?"

"Well, Charlie over there," Gene pointed toward the tree, "needs an oil change and a lube job. Frank, he needs some welding done, and John wants you to detail his wife's car. Can you handle that?" he asked.

"I can handle that, but I don't know what to charge. All I can do is write up the work orders, and you'll have to pay Hank later. That okay with you?"

"Sure," Gene said with a beaming smile. "Maggie said you don't handle any money except gas. We'll just pay her what we think it's worth, if that's okay with you."

In somewhat of a stern voice, Preacher replied, "That's between you, Maggie, and Hank. All I'm doing is keeping a promise. Trying to help a man that needs it. Whatever you do is fine by me. Just do the right thing by Hank."

"Great; when do you want to start?"

"It's not noon yet, so I should have time to do it all today. Let me put some of this stuff back, and let's make Hank some money. I'll take the welding first, the oil change next, and the detailing last. The detailing will take the longest."

"Okay," Gene said in an excited voice. "I'll tell them." He headed for the tree.

* * * * * * *

Maggie had paid attention to the activity around the station. The boys around the tree had questioned her all morning about Preacher. She had commented on the cleaning he was doing, how he wouldn't accept any money for anything but gas, and how he wasn't doing it for pay. He was helping Hank.

When Gene walked in the door of the diner with his work order for the welding Preacher had done, he was as excited as a kid with a new toy. “Maggie,” he said, “I want to pay my bill.”

Maggie looked at him questionably. “You don’t owe me any money.”

“I know. Preacher said we should pay you for the work he’s doing for us. He said to do the right thing. He said to pay what we think the job’s worth.”

Maggie shook her head and smiled. “I don’t know what Hank charges for things.”

“He said we were to pay what we thought was fair. He fixed my muffler, and here’s the work order. Let’s see; he studied the invoice: two exhaust pipe hangers, one clamp, and twenty minutes welding. I’d say that comes to about one hundred dollars. Does that seem fair?”

“Gene, I think that’s more than fair.”

“Good; I’d like to pay it.” He handed her a one hundred dollar bill.

“Okay,” was all Maggie could say. She wrote paid in full and entered the hundred dollars on the total line. “I’ll staple your money to the invoice and give it to Hank. Thank you, Gene.”

“Not a problem,” he said. “Frank, Charlie, and John are bringing in some more work for him too. I’ve got the whole bunch bringing in work to help Hank,” he said as he walked out the door. He had a certain bounce to his step as he strutted over to the tree with his invoice.

I’ll bet everyone over there will pay a hundred dollars before he quits braggin’, Maggie thought. She looked out the window as Frank and Preacher were unloading a rototiller from the back of Frank’s truck. Preacher, she thought, now you’ve got them started, where will it go? They all know that Hank wouldn’t accept charity, but if you do the work, they will pay, and pay generously.

Preacher worked continuously throughout the afternoon. Maggie had been right. When he gave them their invoice, they marched right over to *Maggie’s*. They all paid one hundred dollars. Charlie was the only one to complain. Maggie reminded him that it was for Hank and Tina. He paid his hundred dollars.

Maggie had started to clean up when Preacher walked in the front door. He looked tired. "Well, how did we do today?" he asked.

"Better than I thought," Maggie said as she tapped the top of the jar. It was full.

"You made Hank four hundred dollars in one afternoon," she continued.

"All I said was to pay what they thought was right. Gene's the one that embarrassed them all into the hundred dollars," he said.

"You did well, Preacher. I know for a fact that Tina doesn't have insurance for Josh. This money will help, but it won't pay the bill. They will be paying this one for a long time," she said.

"If I was back at home, I'd call my brothers and put together a poker run. Bikers are always looking for a reason to go for a ride, and if it helps someone, it's even better," Preacher announced.

"The only biker around here is Eddie. He's not much of one, so don't count on him to help."

"Is that the guy in the old truck that owes Hank money?" he asked. She had his full attention.

"That's the guy."

"Well, I can tell you one thing, that dirt bag ain't no biker," Preacher said with conviction.

"Maybe not, but he's trouble."

"There's no 'maybe' to it. He ain't a biker. It takes more than a bike to be a biker. It's a way of life. It's a code of honor. If he causes any trouble here or at the station while I'm here, he *will* answer to me," he stated matter-of-factly.

"Throwing your protective wing over us are ya?" she asked.

"Let's just say I can't stand people that take advantage of the innocent."

Maggie stood and looked at Preacher. "You should be in a western novel. Where do you come up with these sayings?"

"Probably out of the same book they did. It says "Do unto others as you would have them do unto you." If he causes trouble, I think he should get trouble. I like to think that bikers of today are the same as the line riders of that era, men of honor and pride, not trouble," he concluded.

"You're definitely a man of honor and pride. The trouble part is still out with the jury."

Preacher smiled and took her by the waist. "Is that why you took a shine to me?" he asked.

"No, not at first. You were interesting. I hadn't been with a man for a while, and I thought you might be fun. Now, I know you're fun, but that's not what interests me now."

In a sly voice, Preacher asked, "What interests you now?" He put his arms around her shoulders.

She put her arms around his waist. "Chicken; I was thinking of frying some chicken for our picnic. If you don't get out of here and let me do it, you won't get the chicken you asked for." She stood on her tiptoes and lightly kissed him. Then shoved him away. "Now get. I'll be over later."

"I was thinking that I might take a little putt before dinner. What time do you want me back?" he asked.

"It'll take me an hour or so to cook the chicken, so maybe seven or seven thirty. That okay with you?"

"See you then," he said as he started for the door. He called back over his shoulder. "What's for dinner?" he asked.

"Leftovers," she responded from the kitchen.

She heard the old '74 as it roared to life, and then settled down to the distinct throb of a Harley. She didn't go out to look. She knew that today he would come back. She also knew that some day soon, she would hear him leave, and he would not come back.

* * * * * * *

The day had been a long one for Hank. After the doctor had left, excitement filled the air. The anticipation of Josh waking up had given them all a shot of adrenalin. Hope had replaced fatigue. After a few hours, however, fatigue and disappointment recaptured their moods.

Tina and Roy had talked quietly most of the day, their future being the main topic. Roy had all but insisted that Josh convalesce at the ranch where his mother could oversee his recovery. Tina, in her typical forward manner, had wholeheartedly refused. "I'll take care of my own," had been her argument.

"Tina, I'm going to be a part of that boy's life whether you like it or not," had been Roy's rebuttal. Any conflict they might have had, had been solved by Josh.

They had been discussing their future when Josh had moved his legs and groaned. Any animosity they might have had, had been replaced by the protective parental instinct. The nurse had been summoned, and the doctor had been called. Anticipation had returned.

"When we go home, why don't you stay at our house? That way you could watch him while I work," Tina stated.

"Tina, I have a ranch to help run. Dad's not as young as he used to be. Besides, I have my own house at the ranch. Why don't you stay there, and I'll take you to work and pick you up?" Roy had stated.

"Don't you think Josh would be more comfortable in his own bed?" she asked.

"We could move it out to my house. If I had my way, that's where you both would be living anyway."

"Is there a question in that statement?" Tina asked with a sideways glance.

* * * * * * *

"Can I still be your son?" came a small voice from the bed. "I didn't let go. Can I still be your son?" Josh asked in an innocent voice.

Tina and Roy were instantly on their feet, rushing to his bedside.

"Can I?" he asked.
Roy looked at Tina, "I think you'd better ask your mother; she'll be the one to answer that question."
Tina looked at the bandaged body of her son. A smile spread across her tear-streaked faced. She looked up at Roy. She took her stance, with a hand on her cocked hip, and a sassy shake of her head, as she said, "I don't know. I haven't been asked."

* * * * * * *

Hank was sitting in the waiting area when he noticed the activity increase at the nurse's station. The nurses were scurrying in and out of Josh's room. Roy came out of the room, wiping tears from his cheeks. A smile was on his face.
"What's happened?" Hank asked.
"Josh woke up," Roy said. "They asked me to leave until they can check him out. The doctor's on his way."
"Did he say anything?" Hank inquired.
"Yes, he did," Roy said. "He asked if he could be my son."
Hank stopped, looked at Roy, stuck his hands in his pockets and asked, "And?"
"I think the devil just bought a snow cone machine," Roy replied.

* * * * * * *

The feel of his old girl vibrating between his legs excited Preacher. The sensation was not a new one. He always felt the same as he let her warm up. The freedom of the road. The release of tension. His bike found its rhythm. With an audible click of the transmission, the bike lurched forward, only to be held back by the brakes and clutch. Preacher smiled as a twist of the wick had the girl pouncing up on the road to announce her presence. He rolled his hand back and let her have her head. This is what makes a biker, he thought, not the show. It's the freedom of the road. Every junction means a new decision, a new adventure. The wind was warm in Preacher's face. It had been two days since he and his old girl had danced. It felt good.

Maggie had told him to be back in an hour or so. The events of the past few days had Preacher thinking about Hank and Josh. Being delayed was one thing, being stuck was another. He didn't feel bad about what he had done. Sometimes you have to step up and do what needs to be done. Hank had helped with the flat tire and had bought dinner. Preacher had helped Hank. The accident was that, an accident.

Hank had needed him, and he had stepped up. Now, the whole community was helping. *Maggie's* was the central point for the community. It had been her that had helped bring everybody together. It had been inspirational to work for donations and help her. What would the community think if they knew she was sleeping with me, he thought. Smiling, Preacher rolled the throttle back for a burst of speed. It felt good to be on the road again.

Preacher recognized the turnoff Maggie had taken. Slowing down, he took the turn. The pond would be a good place to relax uninterrupted. Rolling up to the rock, Preacher was again struck by the beauty of the oasis. Shutting down his bike and dismounting, he was glad he hadn't dressed in full leather. His scrodie, Levi's, and sleeveless T-shirt were cover enough on an afternoon like this one. The afternoon sun glistened off the surface of the pond.

Sitting on the rock, Preacher thought about the purpose of this delay. Why was I delayed here? What am I supposed to learn? Every junction in life has a purpose. Why am I here?

The entire purpose of this road trip was to decide what path to take for the rest of your life, Preacher thought. He couldn't comprehend the significance of Maggie, Hank, or Josh.

He could, however, understand what time it was getting to be. He needed to get back and shower before he returned to Maggie's for the evening.

Maggie heard the big black bike returning before she saw it. Preacher looked like a warrior riding up to the station. The dark glasses, the cut-off jacket with all the patches and pins, the wolfish grin he had on his face: these all personified the image. Maggie smiled because he looked happier than he had been for two days. No one will ever take him off the road, Maggie thought, he belongs there.

"Preacher," she called.

He looked over as he took off his helmet.

"Do you have any laundry?" she asked.

He nodded his head yes.

"Bring it over with you. I'll put a load in before dinner."

He gave her the high sign as he walked in the front door to unlock the bay door, so he could put his old girl to bed.

Showered and shaved, Preacher gathered up what laundry he had and headed out the back door. Maggie had put the *Closed* sign on the front door, but he had noticed a rear entrance when he was putting Maggie's Malibu away. He walked around behind the building. Maggie met him at the back door.

"Here, give me those dirty clothes," she said as she took the small bundle from Preacher. She was dressed in Levi cut-offs, a midriff tank top, and the moccasins she had worn the previous night. Her hair was brushed out.

"The washer and dryer are here on the porch," she said as she sashayed over to a third screen door between the garage and her back door. "I'll just toss them in now and hang them up later."

Preacher leaned on the door jam and watched her as she loaded the washer. Still no panty line, he thought as she bent down to get a cup full of detergent.

She turned around to find him leaning on the door frame smiling. "What are you smiling about? Was your ride that good?" she asked with a smile.

"Yup, it felt good to go for a little putt. The visual entertainment over here isn't bad either. I was thinking about another ride I'll be taking before we're through."

"Don't get too sure of yourself," she admonished as she slipped between him and the door. "Come on, Romeo, let's eat."

The kitchen was a bouquet of smells. The crisp fried chicken cooling on the counter, the baking powder biscuits from this morning, and a thick hearty stew simmering on the stove. Maggie had set two places at the big prep table.

"Preacher, would you please grab a couple a chairs from the dining room?"

"Sure," he replied.

"What do you want to drink? Beer?"

"No; water maybe, or some of your tea."

"That's three times you've turned down a beer. Don't you drink?" she asked.

"I'll have a beer once in a while, but I prefer water with my meals."

Maggie stood and looked at Preacher. "The more I learn about you, the more I like," she said. "Don't you have any vices other than your marijuana?" she asked.

"Pot isn't a vice, its medicine. In California you can get a script for it. The doctors tried to get me to take valium, but I said no. I asked for an alternative, and they recommended cannabis. Now, instead of poppin' pills or drinking, I smoke. It does the same thing. It relaxes me."

"Well, I hope it gave you an appetite. We've got leftover stew and warmed up biscuits. I've already fed Mom, so let's eat."

The meal was a comfortable one. They talked about Hank and Tina, Tina and Roy, and of course, Josh.

The phone rang as Preacher was wiping the last of the thick gravy out of his bowl with a buttered biscuit.

"I hope that's Tina," Maggie said as she got up to answer the phone. "Hello...Tina! God, it's good to hear your voice; how's Josh?"

Maggie leaned back on the counter and listened. Preacher picked up his bowl, put it in the sink, and headed for the door.

Maggie found him wiping down his bike. Hank's radio was playing softly in the background. She had put on a Levi shirt for the chill.

"Well, Josh woke up," she said.

"That's good," Preacher replied as he continued to clean his bike.

"Do you want to know the first thing he said?" Maggie asked.

"Okay, what did he say?" he replied.

In a broken voice that had Preacher looking at her, Maggie said, "He asked if he could still be Roy's son." A tear escaped her eye and rolled down her cheek. "Can you imagine that, after all he's been through, the first thing he says is that he wants to be Roy's son? Tina was floored."

"It sounds to me like he knows what he wants," he said.

"Yeah, well I hope those two do get together. They're made for each other."

"So, what's the prognosis?" Preacher asked.

The question stopped Maggie. She knew what the real question was. In a more business like voice she replied, "He's still in ICU but should be moved to a ward tomorrow. If all goes well, they should be home Tuesday afternoon."

"Good. I still have a few things to take care of here at the station. I haven't fixed those tires yet."

Maggie shook her head and smiled. "Still making Hank money. What else are you going to do?"

"I don't know. Maybe rape and pillage a local business woman."

"There's only two in this town, and I don't think you would be interested in the other one."

"Then I guess you're on the top of my list," he said as he folded his shop rag and laid it on the seat of his bike.

"Can you at least wait until we get back to my place before you rape and pillage?" she asked. "I'm cold."

"That works for me," he said.

* * * * * * *

"So, this is where you live," Preacher stated as Maggie led the way into her small apartment behind the diner.

"This is the place," Maggie said with a sweep of her hand. "Home, sweet home. It's small, but it's mine. Mom had a Mexican woman that helped her while I was away. She lived here. After Mom got sick and I came back, she went to live with her son, Miguel, out at Gene and Roy's place. I still see her, but she's getting old. Doesn't get out much anymore."

"This place is all one big extended family, isn't it?" Preacher asked.

"We have a few that we're not too proud of, but for the most part, yes."

"Does that go for that Eddie idiot?"

"No! He's from around here, but he thinks he's a gift to this town. Drinks and fights most of the time. Lives with his old man out east of here," she offered.

"And he thinks he's a biker?" he asked.

"He thinks he's something. We haven't decided what he is, but yes, he thinks he's a biker."

"I'll have to meet him someday; that might be interesting."

"Preacher, he's tough. I've seen what he's done to a few of the local workers. It wasn't pretty."

"Maggie, in every crowd there's always an asshole. I'm proud to be a biker. I would do almost anything for my brothers. If this guy calls himself a biker and picks on the locals just because he can, he needs to meet a real one and have the rules explained to him. After what he said to Hank, I would like to be the one to explain it to him."

"Preacher, if you do meet him, watch him. He doesn't play fair," Maggie warned.

"Good," Preacher said, "because I don't either."

"Enough of this talk. I need to go check on Mom. Relax and watch some TV or something. I'll be right back."

The apartment was small, but comfortable. The front room measured about twelve foot square. A well used recliner with an end table and lamp of some vintage occupied the space just inside the door. The far wall was adorned with a small couch and coffee table. Preacher walked through the living room to a short hall that teed into a small, but spotless kitchen. The bathroom was at the top of the T with a comfortable bedroom to the right. The entire apartment smelled of flowers. A woman definitely lived here.

When Maggie returned, she found Preacher kicked back on the couch, with his boots off, surfing the channels.

"Don't you get any sports channels?" he asked.

"I don't know," Maggie replied. "I don't watch sports. I do have a couple of old movies, if that suits you."

"Do ya have *The Outlaw Josie Wales*?" he asked.

"Yes," she said as she hung up her jacket. "Is that what you want to watch?"

"I'm really not a TV watcher. Do whatever you like. I'm easy to please."

Maggie sat next to him and pulled her legs up. "I'm closed tomorrow and so is Hank's. We can do anything we want."

"I heard some rumbling about painting or something tomorrow from Gene. I don't think it would be a good idea if I were to wander out of here too late in the morning," he said.

She sat up and asked. "Gene was talking about painting the station?"

"I think it was you that suggested it. Didn't you say he could paint before breakfast?"

"Yes, but I was only joking."

"Well, I told him if he wanted to help, he could have someone come in and mow lawns. I think he's going to do it. He was pretty excited about helping Hank."

"You've got this whole country anxious to help," she stated. "Gene feels responsible because of Roy."

"Why? Does he feel Roy is responsible? From what I heard, it was an accident."

"It was. Gene is Roy's dad, and Roy was with Josh when he got hurt. That makes it Roy's responsibility, in his book."

"Okay," Preacher said. "I guess that works."

"What time do you think they will show up?" she asked.

"I don't know, but I think it'll be early."

Maggie lifted herself up to her knees and swung one over Preacher to straddle him. She put her hands on his shoulders. "Then I think we should go to bed. It's almost ten o'clock. If you're going to help, and take me on our picnic, you're going to need your rest," she said with a smile.

"And what are you going to need?" he asked.

She swung her leg back over him and stood up. Taking his hand, she pulled him up off the couch. "I'll show you," she replied as she led him to the bedroom.

* * * * * * *

Preacher woke up early. Maggie was wrapped halfway around him, in the same position she had been in yesterday morning.

"Don't move," she whispered. "It's way too comfortable for me to move." She sighed, "I could get used to waking up this way."

"Don't get too comfortable; the sun's starting to come up."

"This is my only day off. I get up everyday at four-thirty. Today, I want to sleep in," she said in a whiney voice.

"Then sleep in. I'm getting up," Preacher said.

"Are you sure?" she asked as she lowered her hand.

"Well, maybe I could spare a few minutes," he said as he rolled over so they were face-to-face.

"I thought you might change your mind," she purred.

* * * * * * *

The sun had barely cleared the horizon when Preacher sauntered out Maggie's door. He had left her in a blissful heap of sheets and blankets. The morning was a glorious one. The sun, still more orange than yellow, reflected off the few white puffy clouds, giving their undersides an almost crimson hue. When he rounded the back of the station, the rabbits stood up at attention, but didn't run. They're getting used to me, he thought. Thinking of the day ahead, he noticed that the green expanse within the white boundary did need to be mowed. Saluting the rabbits with his coffee cup, he ambled through the back door. His black bike had a different look about it with the sun still low in the sky; the luminous paint reflected an almost orange glow. The chrome sparkled.

Opening the bay doors, Preacher noticed the four tires he still needed to fix. He had cleaned the tire machine yesterday. The old machine sat stately in its place. That's eighty dollars of work for Hank, Preacher thought. He put his coffee cup on the bench and started toward the tires.

These tires were not split rims like the ones he had fixed Thursday. These four were all standard rim, tubeless tires. He turned on the breakers for the pumps and the compressor. If Gene and the boys showed up, Preacher didn't want to hinder any effort they might afford. He filled the first tire with air then put it in the tire tank to pinpoint the leak. It had a bead leak. Picking up the tire, he placed it on the tire machine, tightened the collar, and stepped on the foot valve to break the bottom bead loose.

The split rims had to have the ring hammered loose then walked off. These tires were different. He picked up a pipe with a collar welded to one end and a foot about twelve inches above the collar. He placed the collar over the pedestal and used the leverage to break the top bead. After removing the tire, he proceeded to clean the rim. The other three tires were simple patch jobs. Preacher was on the third tire when Gene pulled up.

"Morning, Preacher," he said as he got out of his truck. "I see you're still working."

"I thought I should at least fix these tires. It's worth eighty dollars to Hank. Maggie hasn't counted the money in the jar, but with what you and your friends donated yesterday, and these tires, we've made over five hundred dollars for the kids. You should be proud of your friends and this community for the help they're giving," Preacher said.

"I am proud, Preacher, of you and the community. Everybody wants to help. If it hadn't been for you and Maggie, I don't think anything would have happened."

"You can thank Maggie for everything that's happened. If she hadn't needed her brakes done, I'd be gone. As it was, I helped Hank because he helped me. That's why I'm here," Preacher said.

"Don't underestimate yourself, Preacher. I think you helped in the way you knew how. I couldn't weld that tiller for Frank. Hell, I couldn't weld my own exhaust pipe. You had to."

"All I did was promise Hank that I would stick around until he gets back. I needed something to do. This hasn't cost me anything but time, and time is what I have a lot of."

"Where you going after this, Preacher?" Gene asked.

"I don't know. I have some brothers to visit along the way, but I'm not sure where that way leads," he replied.

"You'll make it to where you're going, son. If you help people along the way, good things will happen for you. We all go out naked and broke, but if someone remembers you, with good thoughts, you're immortal. This town will always remember you. You're history around here, Preacher."

"I don't want to be anyone's history; all I want is the road and a full tank of gas. I'll make my own history," he said.

"Like I said, you made your history around here. Keep doing what you're doing, and I'll call you friend. Now, where are we going to paint? I've got three gallons of white paint and one gallon of red. This is a Texaco station. What needs painting?" Gene asked.

"How about the office and maybe the front, if you have enough paint?" Preacher said.

"Good enough. Some of the boys are going to show up in a bit, and we'll get started. I'll go roust Maggie so she can put on some coffee." Gene headed across the highway.

Preacher watched Gene cross the highway. Maggie must be up by now, Preacher thought. If not, I hope she has some clothes on when Gene bangs on her door.

The sound of a truck caught his attention. It was coming from the west. I'll bet that's one of Gene's boys, Preacher thought. The truck came into view a few moments later. It was being herded down the road by a middle-aged Mexican with an older woman as the passenger. The truck came to a halt next to Gene's truck, and the driver got out. He walked around to the passenger door to open it for the older lady. The next truck came into view as the older woman climbed out of the first truck. A third truck showed up coming from the east. Preacher recognized the two latter trucks. One was Frank's, and the other one belonged to Charlie. He had seen both trucks everyday out by the tree.

Preacher strolled over to the trucks to greet Frank and Charlie.

"Morning, Preacher," said Frank. "Are you ready to paint?"

"I'm not painting. I'm fixin' tires," Preacher responded. "Who came up with the idea to paint, one of you three?"

"Hell, no! Maggie suggested it, and Gene thought it was a good idea. So, here we are," Frank said. "By the way, my wife thanks you for fixin' the tiller. She had me working on the garden spot last night."

"No problem," Preacher said.

Gene came up to the trucks with a steaming pot of coffee. "Anyone want a cup before we start?"

Charlie, Frank, and the Mexican man all held up a cup for Gene to fill. "Maggie said she would bring over sweet rolls later. Preacher, where do you want us to start?"

"Whoa," Preacher said. "Slow down, I'm not the boss."

Gene looked at Preacher with a quizzical expression. "You said you wanted us to paint the office and maybe the front of the building. Isn't that right?" Gene said.

"Yes, but I'm not leading this crew. I'm fixin' flats."

Gene looked at Preacher and smiled, "Okay; Charlie, let's unload the paint; Frank, grab the rollers and brushes. Let's get to painting. Preacher you fix flats."

Preacher smiled back at Gene. "You got it, boss," he replied.

"Preacher, come over here and meet the foreman of the ranch and his mother. Miguel, this is Preacher."

Miguel offered Preacher his hand.

"Preacher, Shasta County, California," he said as he took Miguel's hand.

"You don't look like any Preacher I've ever seen," he said.

"Nor I," said the older lady.

"Preacher, mi madre, my mother."

"I've heard about you from Maggie. The pleasure is mine," Preacher smiled.

"A Preacher should have manners. I'm glad of that. It is good to meet the man that is helping Tina and her family."

"Miguel, take me to the house. I will start cleaning for their return. It is good to meet you, Preacher."

"Lupe!" came a cry from across the highway. "How good to see you."

"Ah, Miss Maggie, how is your mother?"

"Not so good anymore. She will be glad to see you," said Maggie.

"I came to clean Tina's house. Miguel said everybody was helping. I will have tea with your mother when I finish," the stately woman said.

"Good. I will have it ready."

"Miguel, take me to the house."

"Yes, Mother," he responded.

Preacher watched the byplay with interest. "So, that's Lupe?" he asked Maggie as she walked over to him.

"That's Lupe. She is my mom's oldest and dearest friend. I guess when they were both young, they cut a pretty good swath through the men around here."

"She lives with Miguel?"

"Yes. Remember, I told you?"

"Now I remember. She left when you came back?" he asked.

"Yup, Mom retired and so did Lupe. They turned the diner over to Tina and me. Lupe helped raise Tina when Hank's wife died, so she has a vested interest. Now she's cleaning Tina's house for their return; isn't she sweet?"

"I don't know if I could live with her. She's a take charge kind of woman. Miguel must be very tolerant."

"She's his mother. She has earned everybody's respect, especially Miguel's. So how's it going?" she asked.

They both looked back at the station. Gene, Frank, and Charlie were washing down the front of the building.

"It's going," he said.

"Are they going to paint the whole building?" she asked.

"No. Gene said he only had a couple of gallons of paint, so I think they're going to paint the front and the office. I do like the colors though, red and white."

Maggie looked up at Preacher and smiled. "Yeah, I'll bet you do at that."

He looked at Maggie. "Where are the sweet rolls? I didn't get any breakfast."

She blushed, "You were too busy."

"Busy? I was ambushed," he countered.

Maggie squared her shoulders, "Am I going to have to deal with your sweet tooth forever?"

"You don't know, do you?" he said.

"No, we don't," she said as she sashayed across the highway.

"Preacher," Gene called. "How do you want to do this, the same as before?"

"That'll be good. White with a red border."

"Okay," Gene started directing his crew.

Preacher walked back to his tires.

* * * * * * *

Preacher stood up. He had been mixing paint for the crew. Gene had started the stoic renovation with little, or no, forethought. Frank and Charlie had washed the front of the station while Preacher had fixed the last two tires. He had felt it first. The air seemed to vibrate. He stood up from mixing the paint and looked east. Something was in the air. It only took a minute until the vibration evolved into the rumble of multiple Harleys riding as a pack. He had heard this sound many times in his life.

The sun had almost reached its pinnacle for the day when they came into view. The sound became a roar. Preacher moved his old girl out of harm's way as the crew proceeded with the washing and scraping. The bikes thundered down the road side by side. They were traveling. Preacher recognized all of the bikes. They were some of his brothers from Shasta County. The roar followed them past Hank's station only to lessen as they slowed down and turned around. The group was led by a single Hell's Angel. Preacher had parked his bike to the side of the pumps. They stacked theirs along side his. One of the bikes was almost a replica of Preacher's shovel. It was a '75 FLH, jockey shift, with a Scottish family crest on the rear fender. This was the man Preacher engaged first.

"Apache, my brother," he said as he strode up to the group. The rider of the big black bike took off his helmet. Apache was not as tall as Preacher, but he was just as muscular; he was also bald.

"Preacher," he said as they embraced. "What the hell are you doing out in the middle of bum-fuck Egypt?" he asked.

"Helping an old man," Preacher replied.

"Helping him do what?" Apache asked.

"It's a long story. I'll tell you when I get back. Right now I need you to get a message back to Daymond."

"Daymond, what the fuck do you need a lawyer for?"

Preacher told him.

"Okay," Apache said. "I can do that." He continued, "I heard you were going on a road trip, but it doesn't look like you made it very far."

"Like I told you, I got sidetracked," Preacher said.

They talked for a minute.

"Preacher," Apache said, "we'd like to be home tonight, so we won't stay. I thought you might be broke down or something. Now that I know you're just resting, we'll be on our way."

"Top your tanks off here, and get on down the road. You're only six hours out. I owe you one, Apache. I'll see ya when I get back," Preacher said.

Maggie came out of the diner, coffee pot in hand, as the group topped off their tanks. Apache looked over at Preacher and smiled. "If I'd known you had a woman stashed out here, I might have tagged along."

"Maggie," Preacher called, "come over here and meet my brothers."

Maggie looked as good now, in her cut-off jeans and moccasins, as she had last night. She was not shy as she ambled over to Preacher and Apache. "Any friend of yours is a friend of mine," she stated as she walked up to the pair.

"Maggie, meet Apache. That's Red over there..." He introduced her to them all.

"Preacher," Red said, "if you're not broke down, we need to get back on the road."

"I understand; thanks for stopping."

"No problem," Red said.

The thunder exploded as they all fired up their bikes and departed.

"Does seeing your brothers make you home sick?" Maggie asked.

"No," Preacher said. "They all know why I'm here. They understand that sometimes, the wind in your face and the black ribbon of a highway is the only way to get your head back on straight. They will be there if I return. If I don't, they will understand."

"It's good to have some attachment to your roots," she replied. "Are you going to stay and work, or are we still going on our picnic?" she asked.

"It doesn't seem right to leave these boys to do all the work. I feel like I need to stay," Preacher replied.

Hearing the conversation, Gene walked over to Maggie and Preacher. "Take the lady on her picnic, Preacher. We don't need you to finish this painting. Why don't the two of you take the rest of the day off? We'll finish up here and lock up when we leave."

"But..." Preacher started.

"No 'but's,'" Gene said. "You two have done enough. Let the rest of us help." Gene smiled, "Now, go! Before I change my mind."

Maggie smiled and looked at Preacher. "You heard the man, Preacher. Take me on a picnic. Let me go change, and I'll be right back." She called over her shoulder, "We are taking your bike, right?"

"If you want," he replied.

"I want," she said as she headed for the diner.

Okay...Preacher said to himself. A picnic it is. Preacher was chuckling as he walked back to the station.

* * * * * * *

"Well, Josh, how do you like your new room?" Roy asked.

"It's okay," Josh replied. "I didn't like the other one."

"How's the headache?" Tina asked.

"It still hurts, but not too bad. My arm hurts worse," Josh replied.

"We'll call for the nurse if it gets too bad," she said.

"Our little man isn't going to let a little pain slow him down. Isn't that right, Josh?" Roy stated.

"Roy, don't be starting on that macho crap. Josh still has to recover from the last stunt you two tried. I don't know which one of you I should be mad at, but I'm still mad at someone."

Roy smiled, "I think we should try bulls next. Any man that can ride like Josh should ride bulls."

"I'm going to ride your bull if you don't knock it off, Roy Gene. Let's let him heal before he tries again," Tina admonished.

"Does that mean I can still ride?" Josh asked.

"Let's get over this ride before we start on the next one," she scolded.

"Tina," Hank said, "why don't you and Roy go back to the motel and get some rest. You've both been here continually for two days. Go get some rest. I'll stay with Josh."

"Are you sure?" she asked.

"We'll watch some TV or something."

"Will you be okay, Josh?" she asked.

"Yeah, me and Grandpa like to watch cartoons," Josh said, smiling at his grandfather.

"Okay...if you think it's alright. I do need a shower and a change of clothes. Roy, can we go shopping sometime today?" she asked.

"Anything you need to do, we'll do," he said.

"Well, if you're sure, Dad."

"I'm sure," Hank replied.

"See you later, Josh."

"Okay, Mom, see you later. Roy, will you buy me something too?"

"You bet, little man. We'll get you some new duds to go home with. We'll see you later, Hank."

They were holding hands as they left.

* * * * * * *

Preacher walked back to his bedroom. He had been in this little spot in the road for three days. A lot had happened. He had begun to respect the locals. Gene had stood up and taken charge of the old boys; Maggie was taking care of everything else. She would make someone a good partner. He knew that she was getting comfortable with the situation. She also knew he was leaving soon. Preacher didn't want to hurt her, but he had no commitment either. He had told her over and over that he was leaving. With Josh only a couple of days away from coming home, Preacher was getting anxious to get back on the road. The relevance of this delay still eluded him. An old man once told him, "Control what you can control, and to hell with the rest; you can't control it anyway." With that thought in mind, Preacher picked up his scrodie, helmet, and gloves. He thought, I hope Maggie has a helmet or doesn't mind breaking the law.

Smiling, he walked out to his black beauty. It will only take about half an hour to get to the pond, he thought; a picnic would be good. He knew she had fried chicken, and he had asked for potato salad. Maggie would probably take in some sun. Preacher would enjoy the quiet.

Maggie came around from behind the diner. She had changed from cut-offs to Levi's. Her top was partially obscured by the leather jacket she wore. Enough showed to let Preacher know that it was another midriff top. She had a well-used helmet and wore the ever-present moccasins. Her hair was pulled back in a triple tied pony tail. She was carrying a picnic basket. She was devastating. "Well, Preacher, are you ready for a ride?" she asked.

"I'll never turn down an offer like that. Your place or mine?"

She smiled and swatted his shoulder. "Be careful, Romeo, somebody might hold you to it."

Charlie and Frank chuckled in the background.

"I see you've been here before," Preacher said as he nodded toward the helmet.

"A time or two," she replied.

"This might be an interesting afternoon after all," he said.

Charlie and Frank stood up and grinned.

"Let's get out of here, Preacher. These two old farts are having too much fun."

"Not as much as I'm going to have," he replied.

"In your dreams, pal; in your dreams."

Charlie and Frank erupted into laughter.

"Preacher," Charlie called, "you're wasting your time. She may flirt, but that's as far as you'll ever get."

Preacher smiled and said, "Charlie, if I didn't think you were right, I wouldn't go with her. I have a reputation to uphold."

"Yeah, I'll bet you do," Charlie said as he and Frank began to laugh again.

Preacher mounted his bike and kicked up the kickstand. "Load up," he said to Maggie. She slid onto the back seat and settled in. She has been here before, he thought when she moved her pelvis up to meet his back.

The old girl fired up with the rumble of an ol' '74. Easing the clutch, Preacher brought his bike up to the road.

"Ready?" he asked. Maggie just nodded. Excitement sparkled in her eyes. He would give her the same kind of ride she had given him in the Malibu: fast. They roared down the road through the first three gears then settled in as he clicked it back into fourth. He could tell from the tense muscles that she was enjoying the ride. She leaned back as they hit the old girl's rhythm.

The trip to the pond passed quickly. Preacher stopped behind the rock where the dirt road ended. He was again amazed by the serenity of the area around the pond. The stately old flat rock, the sweeping willow trees, and the lush green grass.

Maggie hadn't moved. She stirred as if to move, but only forced her pelvis harder into his back. He felt her shudder. He shut the old black bike down.

"My God, Preacher, I haven't had that happen for awhile," she said as she relaxed.

"And what would 'that' be?" he asked with a smile.

She placed her feet flat on the ground and dismounted. "You know exactly what 'that' is," she said with an unashamed glance.

Maggie placed the basket on the ground, took off her helmet, and loosened her jacket.

"So, I take it that you enjoyed your ride?" he asked.

"If that happened every time I went for a ride, you could be replaced," she countered.

"I don't think so," he said as he kicked down the kickstand and dismounted.

Maggie picked up the basket and walked over to the shade under the willow tree. She placed the basket on the ground and knelt next to it. She opened the basket and took a red and white checkered tablecloth out. She shook it out and arranged it, half in and half out of the shade. Preacher watched her as he took off his scrodie and hung it on the bike's headlight. He had put his helmet on his seat.

Maggie stood up and began to disrobe. The jacket was first, the moccasins next, with the Levi's last. She struck a pose. "Well, what do you think?" she asked.

"I think you're wearing way too many clothes," he replied.

She was only wearing the midriff top and a very small green thong bikini.

"We can remedy that," she said as she stripped off the top. She was tan all over. "That better?" she asked.

"That's good enough for now. I'll take the last part off when I'm ready."

"You'd better be ready when I'm ready, or it will be me raping and pillaging the locals," she said with a smile.

Preacher had come to know her, and her body, well enough over the past few days to not be surprised by her antics. She was a woman that knew how to get what she wanted from her man.

She grabbed a bottle of lotion, sat down, and began applying liberal amounts to her arms and legs.

"Do you want some help with that?" Preacher asked.

"Sure," she said as she flopped face down on the sunny side of the cloth. "Would you do my back?" she asked looking back and up at him.

"No problem," he said as he knelt down next to her.

The sight of her lying naked in the sun was almost more than he could stand. The bare bubble butt, the smooth back and shoulders that were muscular from carrying heavy food trays, and the long firm legs that separated slightly at her center. There's no fat on this girl, anywhere, he thought.

"Use plenty of that sunscreen. With my complexion, tanning is a long slow process."

"I've only known a few redheads, and very few were able to take the sun without burning," he said as he straddled her legs.

"That's what I'm talking about. It's a long slow process."

Preacher began to rub oil on her back. When he brushed his hands over the sides of her breasts, she sighed. When he applied sunscreen to her buttocks, she purred. When he began rubbing the oil up her thighs, she moaned.

"You're one hell of a masseur," she purred. "I think you've got the job."

"I accept," he said as he swatted her butt and lay down beside her.

Maggie folded her arms beneath her head and looked over at Preacher. "Preacher," she asked, "where did you come from?"

"Shasta County, California," he replied.

"I know that, but what are you doing here, in my life? Why? I guess is my question. Why are you in my life at this time of my life?"

"That, my dear, can only be answered by you," he said.

"Why are you here?"

"I told you. I'm on this road trip to get my head on straight. I have to decide what I'm going to do with the rest of my life."

"What happened to make you, you?"

"It's a long story," he said.

"We have all afternoon and tonight. Can't you tell me?"

"Maggie, it's personal. Okay?"

"Okay," she said in a small voice.

"How about you, my lady. Where did you learn to ride a bike like that?" he asked.

"When I was in Reno, I had an old man that was a biker. We had a great couple of years. Some drunk killed him when he ran a red light. He didn't even know what hit him. The drunk didn't remember anything." She rose up on her elbows, "That's why I was impressed when you said you don't drink."

"Booze and motorcycles don't mix," he said.

"That's what he said. Yet, he was killed by a drunk."

"How long ago was that?" Preacher asked.

"About six years ago. When Hank called and told me my mom was sick, I used that as an excuse to come home. I haven't had a full-time man since. It hurts to lose the one you love. Can you understand that?"

"Better than you think. I lost a child to cancer. My wife divorced me cause it was my fault, and I lost everything. Now, I'm trying to put it all back together. Yeah, I know what hurt is. All I want now is peace of mind. The road is where I find it. That's why I'm here."

"How long are you going to stay on the road?" she asked.

"I don't know. Until I find what I'm looking for."

"Will you ever come back?"

"Why would you ask that?"

"Because I'd wait if you asked," she replied.

"Don't wait for me. I only know where I'm at, at the moment. At this point in my life, I don't even know where I'm going. Let alone if I'll be back. Let's just enjoy one day at a time."

"You're right," she said as she jumped up.

"I'm going up on the rock. Care to join me?"

"Sure, lead the way; I like the view."

"A butt man, are ya?" she said over her shoulder.

"Yup," he replied.

* * * * * * *

Maggie was still on the rock when Preacher fell asleep under the willow in the shade. The day had turned out to be rather warm. Not one cloud had marred the bright blue skies. They hadn't talked much. Both were involved with their own thoughts. Preacher could understand Maggie's pleasure when she abandoned the world and found solitude on the rock.

Maggie, however, did not sleep. She wrestled with her emotions. Why am I so attracted to this man? Just when I think I can handle life alone, he shows up. She was fully aware that at first it had been strictly physical. He was a lot better than her toy. Maggie didn't believe in love at first sight, but over the past few days, he had showed her that he was a man of honor and pride. He didn't ask much, but gave it all he had.

He had taken Hank's station and turned it into his own. It was now clean with a new coat of paint. Not many men would have taken on that responsibility when Hank had left. Preacher felt obligated. Hank had helped; Preacher had helped. This man was one to ride the trail with. He would be leaving in two days. She knew she could never hold him. People don't *tell* Preacher what to do, they ask permission.

He would leave when he felt his obligation was completed. If he decided to come back, he would. If not…? Maggie decided she had to help Preacher decide to come back. The sex was great, but sex alone would not hold Preacher. He was like the eagle—free. What was it he had said, "Do unto others"? Maggie sat up on the rock. She looked over at her man napping in the shade. He hadn't even tried to make love to her. He had teased her to the point of frustration, now he was asleep.

"Do unto others," she said aloud. "One day at a time. Well, Preacher, if I only have two days left, I need some memories."

She stood up and climbed off the rock. She deposited her bikini bottom on top of her Levi's. She knelt down and kissed him. His eyes opened immediately. She swung her leg over his and started to undo his belt. Preacher didn't utter a sound as he placed his hands behind his head and gazed deep into her eyes. A smile crept across his face. He asked, "Are you suffering from a heat stroke or something?"

Maggie was unbuttoning his Levi's.

"I'm suffering, but not from a heat stroke."

"Pray tell my lady, how may I be of service to you?" he asked.

"Let me show you," she replied.

* * * * * * *

They returned to town early in the evening. Maggie had to check on her mother. The new paint glistened with the sunset. Gene and the boys were gone. Preacher parked his old girl in front of the first bay door. Maggie slid off the back, gave him a kiss, then went to check on Mom.

Preacher walked around the station to the back door. He stopped at the shower and glanced at Hank's house. The lawns were manicured. The windows sparkled from the sunset. Somebody earned their keep today, Preacher thought.

Entering the back door, he went to the breaker box and shut off the pumps and compressor. The place smelled of fresh paint. He opened the bay door. Preacher wandered out to the pumps, turned and inspected the front of the building. The boys had done a great job. The front of the building reflected the orange of the sunset. He did like the looks of the station, with red borders on new white paint. Red and the boys would be proud. He backed his black beauty into the first bay. As he did, he noticed the office. Gene had left a drop cloth over the desk. When he entered the office, he stopped. The walls were brilliant white with a six-inch red stripe running midway around the room. He folded the drop cloth and left it on the desk for tomorrow. He knew they would all be back to discuss the attributes of their efforts. The office looked immaculate. Hank's not going to even know this place when he gets home, he thought. Smiling, Preacher retraced his steps to the bay and into his room. He pulled a change of clothes from his saddle bags and headed for the shower.

He felt a breeze as he was rinsing his hair and turned to see what had caused it: Maggie. She stood just inside the door, and she was disrobing.

"Girl, you show up at the most opportune times," he said with a smile.

"Glad to see you too," she said as she stepped into the shower.

The shower stall wasn't all that big, but it did accommodate the two of them.

"Are you here to wash my back?" he asked.

"No, I'm here to have my back scrubbed. You put all this oil on me; I think it's only fair that you wash it off. Don't you?"

Preacher put his arms around her shoulders and pulled her close. "So, you think I should wash your back. Okay, but only if you wash mine."

"You got a deal, Preacher," she said as she ran her hands up his back, stood on her tippy-toes and kissed him. He reached around her for the soap. He washed her whole body.

* * * * * * *

"Preacher, would you do me a favor?"

"If I can," he said as he toweled off.

"Would you hand me that bag on the seat?"

"Sure, what's in it?"

"A towel and some clothes. I looked over here a while ago and hoped you were in the shower. I hadn't been in a shower with you yet, and I do like to shower with my man."

He handed her the towel and asked, "Am I *your* man now?"

She stopped drying off and looked at him, "You'll always be my man."

"Now Maggie..."

She stopped him with a raised hand, palm forward. "Don't say it, Preacher. I know you're leaving. I just don't want to hear it anymore. I want to think that if things were different, you would be my man, that's all. God only knows how well we fit together. I've never wanted a man like I want you. You've turned me into a nymphomaniac."

"Is that so bad?" he asked as he pulled on his Levi's.

"Yes; yes it is. I'll compare you to every other man I meet for the rest of my life."

Preacher sat down to put his socks on. "I'll take that as a compliment."

"It is, you jerk. Now hand me some clothes," she said.

"Does this mean I don't get dessert tonight?" he asked from the bench.

"No, what it means is that you damn well better perform every night, and morning, until you do leave, or I'll tell everybody you put your socks on inside out."

Preacher looked down at his feet. Yup, one sock was inside out. "Haven't I told you about my reputation?" he said with a smile.

"Yes, you have. Gene and the boys would have a heyday if I told them you dressed funny." She jumped into his lap. "What do you think about that?"

"I think they would be just as shocked if I told them you needed a shave," he said.

"Okay, truce. I won't tell on you, and you can shave me tonight. How's that for a deal?"

"You drive a hard bargain, Maggie."

"That's not all that better be hard when I want it," she said as she gave him a peck on the forehead and stood to get dressed.

"Don't you ever wear panties?" he asked.

"Not since you showed up," she replied.

* * * * * * *

Hank and Josh enjoyed each other's company during the day, watching TV. They shared lunch. The nurses were friendly and kept Hank's coffee cup full. Josh slept a lot of the time away. Hank wandered through the halls and met an older man that was there with his wife. While Josh slept, Hank spent time with his new friend and his wife. While the wife slept, his friend spent time with Hank and Josh.

Roy and Tina arrived back at Josh's room late in the afternoon. Roy had a concerned look about him. Tina was radiant. She no longer wore her uniform from *Maggie's*. Now she wore a burgundy short sleeved blouse, oven necked, with new blue jeans and black penny loafers. Hank wondered what had happened to change her outlook.

Josh looked up and noticed his mother. "Hi, Mom," he said in a groggy voice.

"Hi, son. How are you feeling?"

"I still have a little headache, and my arm hurts," he replied.

Hank intervened, “They gave him some pain medicine a little while ago. He'll be asleep before long.”

“Have you had supper, Dad?”

“No. We shared lunch and a snack, but that's all.”

“Roy thought it might be a good idea if the three of us had supper together. How's that sound to you?” she asked.

“Sounds good to me. Are we eating in the motel?” he asked.

“No,” Roy said. “There's a smorgie down the street, so we thought we could eat there. We can walk, so we won't have to drive, if that's alright with you.”

“Sure. That sounds fun. We'll stay until Josh falls asleep, and then go.”

“Has the doctor been by this afternoon?” Tina asked.

“Yeah, he said Josh will be released Tuesday morning. He wants one more day of observation, and then we can go home.”

“Are you excited to go home, Josh?”

“Yeah, but I don't think I'll ride that ram.”

“Smart child,” Tina said as she looked up at Roy.

“Are we going to the ranch or home?” Josh asked.

Tina looked back at Roy.

“The ranch,” Roy said.

“The ranch?” Hank asked in amazement.

Tina put her hand on Hank's shoulder. “Dad, we'll talk about it later. Let's let Josh get some rest. Okay?”

“Alright, but this had better be good,” Hank admonished.

They looked at the small bundle of bandages. He was asleep.

They told the nurse at the station where they would be if any emergency came up. The walk to the smorgasbord was a short one. It was on the way that Hank chose to bring up the living arrangements.

“So, you're going to be staying at the ranch, is that right?” Hank asked.

“Dad, we think it would be the best for Josh. We'll move his bed into Roy's spare bedroom, and his mother can watch him while we both work. You won't have time with the station. Roy can bring me in every morning and pick me up in the afternoon.

I'll cook your supper when I get off, and I'll keep your house clean. You go to bed early and get up early. The only thing that will change is where we'll sleep. We think it's best for Josh," Tina explained anxiously.

Hank stopped on the sidewalk and put his hands in his pockets. "I hear a lot of 'we's' in that explanation. What do you have to say, son?"

Roy looked at Tina. She blushed. "Hank," he said, "I would like to marry your daughter."

Hank looked at them both for a long moment. "Are we going to have one of those Reno weddings or what?"

"No, Dad, we're not. I want to be married in the front yard of our house. We want to invite all our friends, and your place would be perfect. There's plenty of parking around the station, and Maggie, Lupe, Roy's mom, and I can fix the food."

Hank shook his head. "Have you mentioned any of this to anyone?"

"Well, no," Roy said. "I thought we should get your blessing first."

Hank looked at the sun, "Tina, honey, we aren't going to have any money to spare. This trip will probably break us. How are we going to afford a wedding?"

Tina let out a terse sigh. "Dad, it's not for a month or more. We'll work something out," Tina said in a frustrated voice. Her tone made Hank smile.

"Roy, do you know what you're doing?"

"I think I can handle it," Roy said with a smile.

"I hope so. I don't want you crying to me because she chewed your butt," Hank said.

"I won't be chewing his butt," Tina replied angrily.

"Yeah, right," Hank replied.

"Okay," he said. "You have my blessing. I just hope you know what you're doing." He shook Roy's hand and hugged his daughter. He continued, "Let's not tell anyone until we get home, if that's okay with you two. I don't want the whole town taking bets on how long it will take before she throws one of her famous fits. That way, I can place my bet. I have the inside track. Now, let's go eat; I'm starving all of a sudden."

* * * * * * *

Preacher and Maggie had walked over to her apartment for the evening. The shower had brought the day to a satisfactory conclusion. Now it was time for Sunday night. Maggie had to get up at four-thirty to get ready for Monday morning.

She knew what was coming. The boys had painted Hank's station, and they would want to crow. She would have to wake up with the chickens.

Preacher sat at the table in her kitchen, listening to her stereo. She favored light country and hillbilly music. Maggie had gone into her bedroom to gather up what few clothes she had worn earlier and had added them to Preacher's; most were oily. She needed to do more laundry.

"Preacher," she called, "would you mind if we had cold chicken and potato salad for supper?"

"No; do you want me to set the plates?" he asked.

"Can you find everything?" She stuck her head out the door of the bedroom to look at Preacher. "If not, I'll do it when I get there."

"Not to worry. A couple of napkins, a paper plate, and we're good to go." Maggie came out of the bedroom. She had changed. The T-shirt she wore was way too large. Her shorts, light blue, hung to mid-thigh. Her feet were adorned with sheepskin lined moccasins. She had pulled her hair up into a loose ponytail, doubled with a clip. Preacher had to smile at the image. How many times, during his marriage, had he participated in this scenario? Sunday night, after a busy weekend, everyone wants to relax and get ready for Monday morning.

"Are you finding everything okay?"

"I think so," Preacher responded. "Chicken in a basket, potato salad on the table." He looked up from the table, "How's that for ambience."

"I think it's great; thanks babe. Want some tea?" she asked as she walked over to the fridge.

Preacher looked up. "That sounds good to me."

"I've had a good day, Preacher; thanks."

"Tis my pleasure, my dear, anything to make the lady happy," he replied.

"You make me happy, Preacher."

"Good; everybody deserves to be happy."

Maggie started fussing around the kitchen getting tea for Preacher and a glass of milk for herself. She asked, "You've had a good day, haven't you?"

"Yeah. I helped the boys and got to see some of my brothers from home. That's a good day," he replied.

She asked, "Didn't you like our time at the pond?"

"How could I not like it? You were there."

She came back to the table with the drinks and sat down. She glanced down at her hands, "I meant what I said at the pond."

"Which time?" he asked.

"When I said I'd wait," she looked up at him.

He sighed, "Maggie, honey, don't go there, please. We've talked this thing to death. Nothing is going to change. I'm going to leave; you're going to stay. I might come back; I might not. Just let it go. What happens, happens." He sat back and looked at her. "Girl, we've only known each other three days. We've had some good times. We have two days left. Let's not get stupid."

Maggie's eyes flashed with anger, "So, you think my waiting is stupid?"

He sat back and put his arms on the table, and in a hard voice he said, "Yes. It's a waste of time. You don't know what's going to happen, and neither do I. If it's meant to be, it will be; if not, it won't. If you want to wait, go ahead, but don't count on me coming back." The tension was thick between them. Maggie and

Preacher were looking into each other's eyes when the phone rang.

"Hello," Maggie paused, "Tina, I'm so happy to talk to someone sensible." She looked over at Preacher. "I was just getting ready to knock Preacher out. No, you're not interrupting anything. We were just sitting down to dinner. How are you doing?" Maggie said with true concern as she walked out of the kitchen into the hall.

Preacher got up from the table and followed her into the front room where he found her sitting on the arm of the couch, listening intently. He shook his head and headed for the door.

"Just a minute, Tina. Preacher, where are you going?"

"Out to smoke; holler when you're through," he said as he walked out the door. Preacher walked over to his room and rolled a joint. She's a good woman, Preacher thought. She's been alone for a few years. It's no wonder she's infatuated. She lost her old man, a biker, now she's sharing her life with another biker. This is comfortable for her. Sharing time and space with someone you care about will make you comfortable; we have been spending a lot of time together. Sex with Maggie is exciting. She is adventuresome and aggressive, but I'm not in love. I like Maggie, and I might stop by if I ever do get back this way. She'll just have to accept that. If not, it's on her. I'll be gone in two days or less.

He saw her walking around the diner from her apartment. She had put on a Levi shirt to ward off the chill. She sat next to him.

"Well, what's the verdict?" he asked as he put his arm around her.

She leaned into him. "They're getting married," she said.

"Who?" he asked.

"Tina and Roy," she said dejectedly.

"That's good, isn't it?" he asked.

"Yes," she said as she sat up, "it's a good thing. They have been walking around each other for sometime now. It's about time they did what should have been done a long time ago. I'm happy for them."

"You don't sound very happy," he said.

"I'm not. They're getting married, and you're leaving. Where does that leave me?" she asked.

"It sounds to me like it leaves you right where you were before I showed up. That's a good thing. You've had some fun. You've helped Hank and Tina. It sounds to me like you'd better get busy planning a coming home party," he said.

"You're not going to talk about it, are you?" she asked.

"No," he said. "I'll talk about a party, but not about marriage. That's a sore subject with me." He continued, "You'll need banners, a barbecue, and some party favors. If you have that stuff, I'll set it up Tuesday before they get home. Let's give them a welcome home party they won't forget."

Maggie stared at Preacher's face, looking for answers. After a few moments, she said, "Okay, hotshot, if you want to throw a party, let's make it a good one. Give me a list of what you need, and I'll order it tomorrow. They will deliver it around ten on Tuesday morning. Can you get it all done by two in the afternoon?" she asked.

"Sure can," he replied.

"Then let's go get a list put together."

"What do you want to barbecue?"

Sitting at the table, snacking on cold chicken, they compiled their list.

Preacher thought for a while. "Something quick, like hot dogs or something."

She added it to the list.

He asked, "Do you have any folding tables?"

"Yes, I do. I have one about eight feet long and a card table. Will that be enough?"

"Should be," he responded.

"Mac salad or potato?" she asked.

"Mac," he said.

"Dessert?" she asked.

"Cake."

"Okay," she said. "What do you need for the banner?"

"Some butcher paper and water colors or a marker of some sort," he replied.

"I can do that," she said. Looking up from the list, she asked, "Is that all?"

"I think so."

"Good, I'll call and leave my order tonight, so they will be sure and have it here on time."

"What time do you have to go to bed?" he asked.

"Around nine," she said as she picked up the phone and dialed.

Preacher stood up and began cleaning up the table.

Maggie hung up the phone. "Okay, that's done. What else do you need?"

"Nothing," Preacher said.

He had deposited the paper products in the trash, along with the chicken bones, rewrapped the cold chicken, and covered the remaining salad. He now stood at the sink, washing the silverware. Maggie came up behind him and wrapped her arms around his waist. "I'm sorry for earlier. I shouldn't have snapped at you," she said.

"All's forgiven," he said.

"I just felt left out," she continued. "With all that's happened, and now Roy and Tina are getting married, I felt like I was being left behind."

"Maggie," he turned around and put his arms around her, "you're not left behind; you're leading this parade. Don't be sorry, be happy. Josh is okay, and Roy and Tina are getting married. Those are all good things. Gene told me that as long as someone thinks of you with pleasant thoughts, you're immortal. I think he's right. You are part of my history now. I will always think of you with pleasant thoughts."

"Don't make me cry," she put her head in the middle of his chest.

"I don't mean to make you cry; I want you to be happy. We've had a great time together. We still have some time together. Let's not waste it. Crying is a waste of time."

She looked up with glistening eyes and a smile. "So, now I'm stupid *and* a waste of time?" she asked.

"Girl, you're not stupid nor a waste of time. Redheads are supposed to be full of fire and emotion."

"You definitely have my emotions."

"Maggie," Preacher said in a stern voice.

"Okay...okay, let's forget the emotion. Let's talk about something else. Like going to bed. The other things I said today, I still stand by."

"And what would they be?" he asked as his hands dropped to her derriere.

"Something about getting laid every night and morning until you leave.

Maggie awoke before the alarm went off. The sound of even breathing told her that Preacher was still asleep. She felt bad that they had disagreed the night before, but she meant what she had said. She was going to wait. She knew, in her heart, that this was the man she wanted. If I could, she thought, I would crawl on that big black bike of his and let him take me wherever he wanted. What would it be like to live with this man—share his home, share his dreams? She knew from experience that bikers spent most of their time on the road, going to or coming from a run. She also knew that they protected the ones they loved. Sometimes with their lives. Being the wife of a biker was a lonely life. They always had something to do, someplace to go. It came with the patch. Preacher didn't wear a patch, but if a Hell's Angel stopped to check on him, to make sure he was alright, you know he has history somewhere. He is one of that crowd. They are brothers. Yes, she would wait. Once you've had the best, the rest is a waste of time. She knew she would always compare every other man to Preacher. Making love to him was sheer joy. They fit together, inside and out. Even now as we lay here spoon-style, with his hand holding my breast, I want him inside me; she smiled at the thought. You little hussy. You haven't even known him a week, and you're already planning your life around him. He's going to leave, Maggie, she thought. He has no intentions of coming back. When he finds his peace, he will stay. You have to find a way to make him want to come back. If you can give him something to care about, he will come back.

She felt him stir, but not wake. His hand slipped down to her waist. I will find something for you to care about, Preacher. I will find a way to bring you back to me. If I can't, how could I ever expect to be your wife?

With that thought in mind, she rolled over on her back. His hand slipped lower. The sex is great, but that alone won't hold him. There are too many women out there offering sex. In any clubhouse you can find a party girl. I don't want to be a party girl. I want to be his other half.

"Preacher…baby, are you awake?"

"No," he said. "This is my subconscious speaking." He didn't open his eyes.

Maggie laughed, "Well, Mr. Subconscious, it's time for me to get up, or I should say it's time for you to get up."

"Why would I want to get up?" he said. "It's you that has a job, not me."

"I guess you forgot what I said yesterday, is that it?"

"You said a lot yesterday, most of which I chose to ignore."

"Ignore," she said, "you chose to ignore me?" she asked.

He opened his eyes.

"Yes, I chose to ignore all that stuff you said about you being left out, about you being left behind. I'll pay attention when you stop talking nonsense."

She bolted up from the bed, "God damn you, Preacher. I was even going to forgive you for all the mean things you said to me yesterday, like 'I don't want to hear it', and 'don't be stupid', and…I'm a waste of your time." She was on a roll, "I'll have you know that I'm nobody's stupid waste of time!"

He was smiling; she was mad. He said, "You look kind of cute all shook up. I'll have to fire you up more often."

She held up her balled up fist, "I have your 'cute' right here, asshole."

"My, my, such terms of endearment. I didn't think you cared," he said.

"You didn't think I cared?" Her voice was rising.

"You know damn well I care, you son-of-a-bitch. Okay, maybe at first you were only my man toy, but now, you arrogant asshole, you've got my heart. So deal with it." She plopped back down on the edge of the bed. "Damn it, Preacher. Sometimes you really piss me off."

She grabbed her pillow and swung it at him. He laughed as he snagged her from behind and pulled her back on the bed.

"Don't touch me," she said as she wiggled up to a kneeling position. "I was just laying there, thinking about making love to you. Wondering what it would be like to live with you. Now I think I'd rather have a dog. They're always happy to see you, and they love you unconditionally. I don't think you even know the definition of unconditional love." She sat back on her legs dejectedly.

"Maybe not, but I did hear something about sex. I do know the meaning of that."

"Fuck you, Preacher. I have a headache; handle it." She moved to get up.

"So, now your word's no good, is that it?" he asked with a smile.

"What!" she screeched as she spun around.

"I remember you saying something about every night and every morning until I leave. I haven't left yet."

She moved like a feline as she crawled back on the bed. "You want sex?" she said in a combative voice. "I'll give you more sex than you can handle, pretty boy. You had better still be standing when I'm through, or I'll use you anyway. I don't want you quitting on me halfway through. You *will* satisfy me, period."

He was smiling as she mounted him. "Okay, if I must," he said.

"Shut up, Preacher, and wipe that silly grin off your face."

"Yes, dear…as you command."

"Fuck you," she said.

"I thought that was your job," he stated.
"Fuck you," she said as she began to grind.

* * * * * * *

"Do you want some coffee?" Preacher called from her small kitchen.

"Yes," she replied tersely.

The session in bed had been an arduous one. She had shown the tenacity of a woman on a mission. He had only to lay there and watch her work herself into a frenzy. After she reached her completion, twice back to back, she crawled off him, without saying a word, and stomped into the bathroom.

He had gotten up, pulled on his Levi's, and gone into the small kitchen to make coffee. He recalled the events in his mind. She had it all figured out. She was going to be his wife. I've had about all the wives I can handle, he thought. She would be fun to live with though. Her red-haired temper could be exciting. It could also get old. Yes, Maggie, he thought, I've had about all the wives I can afford. I don't want to hurt you; you're a good woman, but I don't need any clinging vines either.

"Here you go," he said as he handed her the coffee.

"Thank you," she replied as she set her coffee on the shelf under the mirror.

"Are we still upset, my little angel?"

She spun around. "Preacher, don't go there. Yes, I'm still upset, so get out of here." She turned back to the mirror. "I have to get ready for work, unlike somebody else."

He leaned against the door jam. "My, my, you are upset."

"Damn it, Preacher, you hurt me."

"I didn't know I was that good."

She stopped, put her hands on the sink, and lowered her head. "Preacher, you hurt my feelings."

He walked up behind her and put his hands around her waist. "I'm only trying to lighten up the mood."

"Yeah, well, I'm still disappointed."

He pulled her back against him. "I didn't mean to hurt you. You're a good woman. I just don't want to give you any false hope. By this time Wednesday, I'll be leaving," he said.

She sighed and laid her head against his chest, "And not coming back?" she said.

He turned her around. "Maggie, here's the deal. If you see me before the snow flies, we'll talk about it. If not...I won't be back. That's the best I can offer."

"You mean you might come back?" she asked anxiously.

"You heard what I said."

"So, now you're offering me that false hope?"

"It's the best I can offer right now," he said.

"Then I'll wait, but only until the snow flies," she said. "After that, you're on your own. Deal?"

He kissed her forehead. "Deal," he said.

* * * * * * *

Preacher walked over to the station a little before seven a.m. Maggie had made him one of his favorites, a fried egg sandwich with sweet pickle relish. She had commented on the need for a better start for the day. "If you're going to work today, you'll need more than a sandwich," she had said. It had been amazing to watch the transformation she had gone through after hearing his deal. She became more confident of his returning. Her arrogance had returned.

Charlie and Frank had stopped by on their way to Fallon about six-thirty. Maggie had been in top form as she bantered with the two old regulars. When Preacher walked out from the kitchen, they had looked inquisitively, but didn't comment. When Maggie brought out Preacher's folded laundry, it was too much.

"Preacher, Maggie flirts with everyone, but I've never seen her do any man's laundry. Just what did you do out at the pond anyway?" Frank asked.

"I'll never tell—I do have a reputation to protect."

Charlie and Frank had to laugh when Maggie turned crimson and immediately rushed into the kitchen.

"How long are you going to stay, Preacher?" Frank asked.

"Until Hank gets back, you knew that," Preacher said.

Frank continued, "We were thinking that if a man had a truck, and was somewhat mechanical, he could put a welder in the back with a generator and compressor. He could make a good living around here. I know that some of my equipment could stand a good going over."

Preacher was sitting at the counter, looking through the service window at Maggie while Frank made his presentation.

She had looked up with a hopeful smile. When she handed him his sandwich and made her concerns known, Charlie had made the statement, "Maybe I should take my old lady out to that pond, if it will make her treat me like that." Maggie and Preacher had both laughed.

Now looking at the station, as he munched on his sandwich, Preacher felt a moment of pride. The crew had done a fantastic job on the front of the station. The only thing that was lacking was the pump area. That will be my first order of business: paint the island, he thought. He walked around the building to the back door. The green expanse of Hank's front yard had more rabbits than usual. Must be the fresh cut lawn, he thought, as he saluted them with what remained of his egg sandwich. He entered the station and was again assaulted by the smell of fresh paint. After putting his laundry on the bed that he had only used twice, he flipped on the switches for the pumps and compressor. After opening the bay doors he turned around and surveyed the station's interior. His old girl seemed happy where she sat majestically in the first bay. The bays seemed unbalanced. Preacher smiled as his eyes settled on the small blue BMX bike. Preacher grabbed the bike from the wall and placed it in the middle of the second bay. Now you're balanced, he thought. I should get with the painting before long, so it has a chance to dry today. Tomorrow will be a busy day, he thought.

He walked into the office. The drop cloth caught his attention. That will work, he thought. He spotted a couple of paint cans. He picked them up to feel how much paint they held. The white can held little, but the red one was about a quarter full. Leaving them there, he went in search of a paint brush.

Charlie and Frank came out of *Maggie's* and started over to the station. Frank said, "What are you doing, Preacher? You look like you've lost something."

"I haven't lost as much as can't find. I'm looking for one of those paint brushes you used yesterday."

Charlie chimed in, "They're around back, behind the bathrooms."

"Thanks, Charlie."

Frank asked, "What do you need a paint brush for? Didn't we do a good enough job?"

"Oh, no, you guys did one hell-of-a-job. I wanted to paint the island."

Charlie said, "They're in a bucket with some water in it."

"Okay, thanks," Preacher responded.

"You need anything from town?"

"No, thanks," said Preacher. "I think I have everything I need. Thanks again."

As Frank and Charlie walked over to the truck, Frank said to Charlie, "When he first came into town I was a little worried, now I hope he stays. That man is a worker."

Charlie chuckled and responded, "He's a drifter. There's only one thing that would keep him here." They both looked at each other and said in unison, "Maggie."

"Did you see her blush this morning?" Charlie said.

"Yup, I did," said Frank. "I think that maybe they did do more yesterday than picnic and swim. That's good. I like him."

Preacher walked out to survey the pumps. They needed to be washed and scraped. Okay, he thought, this will be something to do for the morning. He went looking for a scraper and wire brush. Hank's tool boxes confronted him. Two top boxes sat on the workbench, side by side. A roll-around rested next to the welding cart in the corner. I should have washed them when I washed the bays, he thought. Looking in the top of one of the top boxes on the bench, Preacher found a scraper. He found the wire brush in the roll-around.

When Gene pulled up to the tree, Preacher was on his hands and knees scraping and brushing the concrete base of the pumps.

"I see we forgot something," he said as he walked up to Preacher.

"You boys didn't forget anything. Hank won't even recognize this place. I needed something to do today, so here I am. Could I use that drop cloth later?" he asked.

"Not a problem," Gene said.

"Gene, you might want to go over and talk to Maggie. She said something about a party tomorrow."

"What kind of a party?" Gene asked.

"A coming home party for Josh."

"When I talked to Roy last night, he said they should be home around two tomorrow afternoon. He said he had a surprise for us. Do you know anything about it?" Gene asked.

"I don't talk with the kids; Maggie does. They usually call around supper time. All I do is eat," he replied.

"You're spending an awful lot of time with that girl; how's it going?" Gene asked.

"It's going," he responded.

"She's a good woman, Preacher. You could do a lot worse."

Preacher looked over at Gene. "I'm leaving Wednesday morning. I'm not looking for any commitment. Hell, I'm not looking for anything. All I want is to get on down the road."

"As good as you weld, you could make a good livin' around here fixin' equipment."

"Have you been talking to Charlie and Frank?" Preacher asked.

"We talked some yesterday; why?"

"They said the same thing. Gene, I don't want a job. I have all the responsibility I need."

Gene sighed, "I suppose you don't need the money either."

"No, I don't. I have enough to get me where I'm going."

Gene shook his head and smiled. "Well, you can't fault us for trying. You're a good man. If you change your mind, we'd welcome you. Maggie might like it too."

"Now, why would Maggie like it?" Preacher asked.

"I don't know about the rest of these boys, but I haven't seen her this happy in a while. If she's interested, you must've done something."

Preacher asked, "So you think Maggie's interested, do ya?"

Gene smiled, "Let's put it this way, you're the only man I've ever known that has gone with her to that pond. I know a few that would like to, but she won't have anything to do with them. Yeah, I think she is interested."

"Well, interested or not, I'm leaving Wednesday," Preacher stated.

"You're missing a chance at a good woman," Gene said.

"Probably." Preacher went back to work.

Gene just shook his head and headed over to *Maggie's*. The first thing he said as he entered the diner was, "Maggie, how come you haven't talked Preacher into staying on around here?"

"Well, good morning to you too, Gene," she said. "Want some coffee?"

"Yes, I do," he said as he took his place at the counter. "You should work your wiles on Preacher and get him to stick around. He's a worker. He doesn't even slow down. Now he's painting the base around the pumps. I wonder what he's going to do next—pave around the tree?"

"He is a worker, that's for sure," Maggie said. "As for him sticking around, I don't think anybody could influence him. He's got something to do, and he's going to do it. He told me last night that if he does stop back by, it will be this fall. I wouldn't count on him coming back before then."

Gene looked questionably at Maggie. "You spent the night with him?"

Maggie squared her shoulders and said, "Yes, I did; I fed him supper; I did his laundry, and we watched some TV. We can't expect him to sit over there at that station all by himself, can we?"

Gene stopped his coffee up about midway to his mouth. "Well, when you put it that way, no, we can't."

Maggie nodded. "I liked the company, and I think he did too. Now don't you go starting any gossip. I don't think he's a man to trifle with."

Gene nodded, then said, "Judging from the fellows that came through yesterday, I wouldn't mess with any of that crowd. I'd have liked to see how Eddie would handle those boys."

Maggie turned around after putting the coffee pot on its warmer. "I haven't seen Eddie since Thursday. Maybe he's smart enough to leave Preacher alone."

Gene smiled, "That would be something to watch, wouldn't it?"

Maggie gave him an impish grin. "Preacher would wad that piece of trash up and put him where he belongs."

"It might be fun to watch, though, wouldn't it?"

"No," Maggie said. "Preacher would hurt him, and I know he doesn't want any trouble, but if Eddie tries something, it will be his fault, not Preacher's."

"Well, if he won't stay, then all we can do is wish him luck and hope he comes back. You'd like that, wouldn't you, Maggie?"

"Yes, I would," she responded.

"I thought so." Gene paused a moment. "Preacher said something about a party tomorrow. What's that all about?" Gene asked.

Maggie smiled; she knew Gene suspected something had happened yesterday. "Last night after Tina called, Preacher said we should throw a coming home party for Josh. I thought it was an excellent idea."

Gene looked into her eyes, looking for answers. "A party, huh? Where?" he asked.

"Over at the station. Preacher said he would barbecue hot dogs. I'm making macaroni salad and a cake. We'll set up tables, and people can serve themselves. We'll set the donation jar on the table and give it to Hank when we're done."

Maggie and Gene were alone in the diner. Gene looked at Maggie and asked, "Is there more to this story that I don't know?"

"I don't know. You talked to Roy; what did he say?"

"He just said they would be home tomorrow."

"Well then, you know as much as we do."

Gene smiled again. "Maggie, I hear a lot of 'we's' coming from you. You be careful. That man would be one to ride the trail with, but it may cost you something to get that ride, if you know what I'm meaning."

Maggie's face softened with Gene's concern. "Preacher and I have become friends. He's a good man, but a hard one. He laughs easily, and I suspect he would fight just as fast. I know who Preacher is, and I would absolutely love to share a life with him, but he's leaving Wednesday morning. He has something to do, and he will do it. That's the type of man he is. If he comes back to me, so be it; if not, I'll have the memories."

Gene placed a hand over Maggie's. "You deserve a man like that. I hope he comes back."

"Me too," Maggie said as she looked out the window at Preacher, on his hands and knees, scraping the paint off the island.

* * * * * * *

The morning was a magnificent one. Pale blue skies, a few high fluffy clouds, and the yellow orb that had not yet turned up its heat. Preacher had a few gas customers early, but they had dwindled as the Monday morning sun progressed along its arc. The island was scraped and washed. He wanted it to dry prior to painting. He wound up the hose and put it in its place. He had to chuckle at the different look the old station had taken on. All of the morning customers had commented on the "face lift". Preacher returned the scraper and wire brush to their respective tool boxes. Maybe this afternoon I could straighten this mess up, he thought.

He heard the truck pull up and looked out to see who it was. He didn't recognize the rig, but he did recognize John from the other day.

"Preacher," he called.

"In the shop," Preacher called back.

"Ah...there you are," John said. "This is a friend of ours, and he needs some welding done. Do you have time?"

"Sure," replied Preacher. "What ya got?"

"Well," the friend said, "it's an old plow shear that my wife wants me to put our mailbox on."

Preacher walked out to the truck to look. He had seen mailboxes mounted on old shears before and had an idea of how to mount it. "Yeah, I think I can do that. Are you going to set it in cement?" he asked.

"That's what I was thinking," the friend said.

Preacher opened the tailgate and pulled the plow toward him. "Do you have any metal for a stand?"

"Well, no," he said.

"I'll have to look out back and see what Hank has, but if he has what we need, I should be able to fix something up for you. Do you understand the drill?"

The friend looked questionably at Preacher. "What drill?"

"I don't take money for the work I'm doing. You pay Maggie—that's the drill."

The friend was visibly shaken. "How much is it going to cost me?"

"That is up to you. Whatever you think is fair. Hank must be a friend."

The man nodded his head.

"So, pay what's fair, but pay Maggie, not me."

"Yes, sir," the friend said.

Preacher continued, "Did you have any ideas as to what you want?"

"Well, no."

"Do you know what your wife wants?"

"Well, no."

Preacher was smiling by this time. "Do you know what day it is?"

"Well, yes."

"Okay," Preacher said, "I think I can help you. When do you want it done?"

"Uh, this afternoon?" he asked.

Preacher picked up the shear and held it. "You got it. Come back around noon, and we'll see what you think."

"Well, okay. See ya," the friend said as John and he got back in the truck. John was laughing.

"What are you laughing at?" the friend asked somewhat perturbed.

"You," John said. "I haven't seen you that rattled in a long time."

"I'm not rattled! I just couldn't think. That man scares me. Who is he anyway?"

"He's the biker everybody's talking about. He's here helping Hank while he's in Reno with his grandson."

"Is he as mean as he looks?"

"I don't know," John said still chuckling. "He hasn't done anything to upset anyone yet, but you'd better pay Maggie. I wouldn't want him mad at me."

Preacher was smiling when he carried the plow back to the station. These people don't know what to think. Am I a good thing, or have they let a cougar loose in the sheep herd? He set the plow inside the bay and picked up the drop cloth and the can of red paint. First things first, he thought as he headed back to the island.

He painted the edge of the island red. Next, he painted the tower that housed the air and water hoses. He washed out the brush. He picked one out of the bucket that had been used for white paint yesterday and grabbed the can of white paint. He painted the deck of the island white. After cleaning the brush and folding the drop cloth, Preacher strolled over to the plow. He smelled her before he noticed her.

"Excuse me, could you help me?"

Preacher turned around and looked into the deepest blue eyes he had ever seen. The woman that stood before him was gorgeous. She was about 5'5" with shimmering blonde hair that hung below her very trim waist. Her tank top was pale blue, and it was tucked into a pair of short shorts that matched. Her legs were trim, yet muscular. Her erect nipples showed Preacher that she wasn't wearing a bra. "If I can't, I'll have to try harder," he said.

She giggled, "I don't think you would have to try too hard."

"Okay, now I'm hard. What do you need?"

"A man," she said as she put her hands behind her back forcing her nipples to stand out even more.

"And what do you need this man for?" he asked.

With a sly look, she grinned and said, "Well, you see, my car has a flat tire, and I was wondering if I could get you to help me."

Now Preacher was grinning. He had played this game before. "I'm here to service those in distress, or undress, whatever the case may be. Where is this car?"

She was swinging her shoulders back and forth like a younger girl would. "It's over there, under the tree."

"Let's go look, and see if I can help." Preacher looked over at the diner in time to see the curtain drop.

"Okay," she said as she led the way.

Following her to her little white sports car, Preacher noticed that the rear view was every bit as enticing as the front. No panty line.

Reaching the little car, she struck a pose by jumping up and resting that rear view on a fender and extending her hands back to rest on the hood. Preacher was enjoying this game of who does what for whom, and how much it will cost. Preacher walked around the car. "Do you have a spare?" he asked.

"I think so. Look in the trunk." She held out the keys.

Preacher brushed his hand lightly over hers as he took the keys from the little vixen. He opened the trunk. The first thing he noticed was the lack of suitcases. Well, she's not traveling, he thought. Under the carpet he found the spare. It glistened with newness. "Yup, I can take care of you," he said.

"I wish you would," she said. "I hope it won't take too long."

"Not long at all," he said. "Let's go back to the station and discuss the price."

She lowered her eyes and smiled. "Okay," she said as she lowered herself off the fender and started toward to the station.

Preacher glanced over at the diner. The curtains, again, fell back into place. He smiled. Upon reaching the station, Preacher walked into the office, grabbed a work order off the back shelf and sat down at the desk.

She cocked one hip up on the corner of the desk next to him and extended the other long smooth leg out in front of her and off to the side. He had the full view. She asked, "So, what's this going to cost me? I don't have a lot of money."

Preacher laid the work order on the desk. "Then maybe we could talk about a little trade, you know, the barter system?" He placed his hand on her knee.

"I don't know what I have to trade," she said in her small voice. Her eyes were as big, and as innocent, as a fawn.

Preacher smiled and said, "I'll tell you what. You do me a little favor, and I'll change your tire. No charge."

She cocked her head and asked, "How little of a favor?"

Preacher got up and took her by the hand, "Come on and I'll show you," he said as he headed out the front door toward the diner.

"Why are we going over there?" she asked as he pulled her along.

He slipped his hand around her waist. "You'll see," he said.

Preacher held the door for the blonde as they walked in the diner. Maggie was standing at the counter. She was not smiling.

"Maggie, honey, this young lady wants to donate twenty dollars to Josh."

The blonde looked back at Preacher and asked, "Who's Josh?"

Preacher bent down to whisper in her ear. "He's my little friend that's in the hospital, and you're going to do him a little favor by donating twenty dollars," he said matter-of-factly. He stood up, "Mag, would you show this lady the donation jar and buy her a soda, please? I have a tire to change."

Maggie was smiling as she placed the jar and a soda in front of the blonde. "That will be twenty dollars, please," she said.

The blonde smiled at Maggie and said, "Well, it's not the deal I expected, but if it's for a good cause." She slipped two fingers in the waist band of her shorts and extracted twenty dollars. As she handed the twenty to Maggie, she asked, "Is he your man?"

Maggie dropped the money into the jar and looked up with amusement in her eyes. "Yup, he's all mine."

Preacher was putting the flat in the trunk as the blonde came out the door of *Maggie's*. Preacher held the door open when she arrived.

"It's not the deal I had in mind when we were talking trade," she said as she settled into the driver's seat.

"Sometimes you win; sometimes you don't. Thanks for the donation."

She looked up and said, "Maybe I'll see you around sometime."

"Maybe," he said as he closed the door.

Maggie came out of the diner when the little white car was back up on the highway.

Preacher was putting the jack and the T-wrench in its proper place.

She asked, "Well, did you enjoy yourself?"

"Sure, a little eye candy will always make the day go better," he responded with a grin.

She swatted his shoulder, "Don't you go having too much fun with the customers, you hear me?"

"Yes, dear," he said as he grabbed her by the waist. "I noticed you watching," he said as he lightly kissed her.

"I wasn't watching," she said as she wiggled to break his hold.

"Yes, you were," he admonished. "I saw the curtains fall."

She kept struggling, "I was just looking to see if you were busy," she said.

He smiled, "Yeah, right."

"Well, I was," she cried.

He shook his head. "You mean that I went through all that and you didn't even notice? I saw the curtains move twice," he said.

She had quit struggling. "Well maybe I did notice her outfit," she said.

"So did I," Preacher said, trying to hold the laughter inside.

She swatted his chest; "Jerk," she said.

"So you were jealous," he stated.

"No, I was not."

"Yes, you were."

"Okay, maybe a little," she resigned. "Just don't be flirting with every half-naked woman that comes down that highway. I can take you out of commission, you know," she stated.

"Are you laying claim?"

She reached up and framed his face with her hands. "Yes, I am," she said as she lightly kissed him. "Now let me go. You have work to do, and so do I. What do you want for lunch?" she asked.

"You," he said.

"I was talking about eating," she said as she pushed herself clear of his grasp and headed for the door.

"So was I," he said as he swatted her butt.

"You're impossible," she said as she left.

Preacher watched Maggie as she strolled over to the diner. Preacher, he said to himself, you're going to have to come back and visit that lady someday. He was smiling when he looked down at the plow shear. He stood it up and began looking at it for a possible design.

If John's friend is going to put this in cement, I will have to weld some J-bolts on the bottom and put a plate on the top for the mailbox. With that thought in mind, he headed out the back door to look through the pile of old parts and metal. He found the plate first. The bolts took some time. Taking the parts back into the station, he looked over at the welding tanks. I'll need an arc welder for this job, he thought. He went looking. He found the welder and a Lincoln buzz box under the bench. Pulling out the leads, he began formulating his idea. He heated the bolts with the torch and bent them into an L-shape. Next he retrieved the wire brush from the roll-around and began cleaning up the plate. When the plate was somewhat clean, he found the center line. With a punch, he set two spots for the holes to anchor the box to the plate. He walked over to Hank's mailbox to get the dimensions for the plate. He cut the plate to size with the torch and then drilled two quarter-inch holes. With a four-inch grinder he ground the edges smooth. Now it's time to weld, he thought. He was just knocking off the slag when John and his friend returned.

"Is this what you had in mind?" Preacher asked.

"That'll work just fine," the friend said.

"Good," Preacher said. "If you'll go eat some lunch while I paint it, you'll be ready to go."

The friend said, "So what do I owe you?"

Preacher looked at John questionably, "Didn't I explain the deal?"

"Well, yes," the friend said.

"Then pay what everybody else pays." With exasperation in his voice, he continued, "All I ask is that you pay Maggie what you think it's worth. That way Hank and Tina will have some money to offset the cost of this hospital visit. I'll bring over the shop order after I paint this thing. Is black okay?" he asked.

The friend asked, "Is that the only color you have?"

"Yup, that's the only rattle can I can find, black primer."

"Then I guess it'll have to do," said the friend.

"Good," said Preacher.

Prior to cleaning up the mess, after building the mailbox, Preacher pulled the tire rack into the second bay. He had noticed that some of the welds had cracked on the pipe rungs. He ground the welds down with the four-inch grinder and re-welded them. Once the slag was knocked off and the metal had cooled, he pulled it over to the gravel and started painting. Preacher hated to paint, but if you're going to do a job, do it right, or don't bother, he thought. He had taken it upon himself to clean the station up as much as possible. The tire rack was an eye sore against the fresh white paint of the station's face. It needed painting. Red was what he had the most of, so red was what it got painted.

He still couldn't conceive the reason he had been delayed in this little spot on the highway. He believed that everything has a purpose. Painting gave him time to think. Looking back on the events of the past few days, he called it running the tapes; he could not find any rhyme or reason for the delay. He had done what was the right thing to do. Hank had helped him. He had helped Hank. He didn't think that standing up for what you believed was the right thing to do was a lesson he needed reinforced. That value was an imperative in his life. "Do unto others as you would have them do unto you" was a standard he lived by. If you give trouble, you get trouble. If you help others, others will help you. Maybe these people had a purpose later in his life. Maybe it was just the luck of the draw. The community had accepted him for what and who he was: a biker. They held no animosity toward him. They wanted him to stay. Maggie wanted him to stay.

Maggie—sweet, sweet Maggie, he thought, maybe you're the reason I'm here. Maybe she has a lesson to teach. Her voice brought him back to reality.

"Preacher, are you ready for some lunch?"

Preacher blinked his eyes. "I don't think so, not yet anyway. Thanks."

"Where were you?" she asked.

"Just running the tapes," he responded.

With a puzzled expression, she asked, "Running the tapes, what's that?"

"It's when you look back on an event and try to decide if you did the right thing or not," he responded.

"I won't ask what brought that on, but I think that tire rack is finished."

Preacher looked at the configuration of pipes. He didn't remember painting the last rung.

"So, what are you going to do for the rest of the afternoon?" she asked.

"Keep cleaning," he said.

"Why don't you go for a ride? Hank puts up the *Closed for Lunch* sign and goes home sometimes. You don't want any lunch, but I'll bet you could use a ride."

He smiled at her, "Maybe this afternoon *we* could go. I want to clean those tool boxes today. If I'm going to put Hank into shock, it may as well be complete. Those top boxes are a mess."

She shook her head and said, "You're a puzzle, Preacher; you are a puzzle."

"What do you mean by that?" he asked as he put the lid back on the paint can.

"I suggest you take a ride, and you don't go. That's puzzling."

"It doesn't feel right to just shut down the station and take a ride. I'd feel like I was cheating Hank."

"My God, Preacher, after all you've done for him. You would feel like you're cheating him?"

"It doesn't feel right, Maggie; it's not the right thing to do."

"Well then, why don't you just relax or play with your bike. You've done enough."

"I might later, but I'm still going to clean up those boxes. I have a feeling you're going to have me hustling tomorrow."

She smiled, "I won't be too hard on you."

"Good," he said; "because I have a feeling tomorrow isn't going to be a joyride for either of us."

The afternoon did go by slowly. Preacher had cleaned up the mess from welding and had put the empty paint cans in the trash. The station was again clean except for the tool boxes. He decided it might be a good idea to hold his own safety meeting.

He went into his room and rolled his medication. Now, it was time to clean tool boxes. With a shop rag moist with solvent, he began wiping the boxes down.

* * * * * * *

Maggie showed up at mid-afternoon. She arrived with a sandwich wrapped in a napkin on a paper plate, and a tall glass of iced tea. "Hey, good lookin'," she said as she strolled into the bays. "Are you hungry yet?"

Preacher turned around to greet her. "I thought you'd never ask. What ya got there?" he asked.

She smiled, "A grilled tuna salad sandwich and your iced tea."

"That'll work," he said as he wiped his hand off on a shop rag.

She placed the sandwich on the bench and handed him his tea. "So, you're still cleaning, are ya?"

"Everything in its place," he said.

She leaned against the workbench. "Are you just as fussy about your home?" she asked.

"I was, when I had one."

Startled, Maggie looked at him in amazement. "You mean to tell me you don't even have a home to go back to?"

"Oh, I have a couple of acres with a trailer on it, but it's not a home. It takes a family and a dog to make it a home."

"Is that what you're looking for, a home?"

"I don't know what I'm looking for. All I know is, it's time to start over. I lost everything in the divorce. Now, I have to figure out what to do with the rest of my life. I don't know if that includes a home or not. That's why I came on this road trip: to figure it all out."

"You could have a home here," she said.

Preacher looked sideways at her, "Maggie," he warned, "don't go there."

She raised her hands in submission.

"Okay, okay, I won't go there."

He continued, "Most of my brothers live and ride in northern California. I would suspect that when I do get my head on straight, I'll go back. When, I don't know."

She was looking at him when she asked, "I noticed all of your friends had the same little UBNC patch like yours. Is that who you ride with, the UBNC?"

"Maggie, UBNC stands for The United Bikers of Northern California. It's a nonprofit corporation, and yes, I ride with them. They donate a lot of money to a lot of organizations. I'm proud to be a member; it makes me feel good to help others."

She smiled at him. "I can see how you help others. Look at this station. I hope that when you do find what you're looking for, you think about me."

"I'm thinking about you right now. Wanna go mess around?" he smiled as he looked over at her.

"Later, big boy, later. I haven't closed up yet, and it looks like I've got a customer. See ya later," she said as she walked out of the station.

Preacher worked on the tool boxes the rest of the afternoon. He was just finishing wiping the boxes down, again, when Maggie showed up. She had changed out of her uniform. She was now wearing Levi's, a tank top, and her moccasins. She had one hand holding her leather jacket, thrown over her shoulder. Her other hand was occupied with her worn helmet.

"What do I have to do to get a ride on that bike of yours?" she asked as she sashayed into the first bay.

"Are you interested in a trade?" he asked with a smile.

"As long as it's not going to cost me twenty dollars," she replied.

He put the folded shop rag on top of one of the top boxes and said, "I think we can find another commodity to trade. That is, if you're interested."

She took her stance. "And what commodity were you considering?"

Preacher smiled, "Ass, grass, or cash—nobody rides for free."

She beamed at his humor, “We’ll talk about your reward when we get back. I want to go for a ride.”

“Anything for a lady,” he said as he walked over to his room. He twisted up a hooter, slipped on his scrodie, and grabbed his helmet. “Which way today, my lady?” he asked.

“West,” she said; “there’s another place I want to show you.”

He pushed his big black beauty out the door and closed it.

“Load up,” he said as he started the beast.

“About twelve miles from here, turn left at the wye in the road. I’ll direct you from there.”

“Okay,” he said as he released the clutch.

He felt her settle in as he hit fourth gear. He rolled the throttle back. His black beauty jumped ahead with a roar of thunder. At the wye, Preacher turned left. Maggie leaned forward and told him where to turn. He turned on another gravel road. It didn’t take long until she was tapping his shoulder. She pointed to a vista, and Preacher slowed to a stop. With his bike still idling, Preacher took in the panoramic view. When he shut his bike down, he didn’t say a word. Words could not describe the view. Most people see the desert as a barren place filled with snakes and cactus. In May, before it gets really hot, the contrast of colors is extraordinary. The crimson red to tawny brown, the pale yellows to dull orange, the vibrant green to the pale green of new leaf. From this vantage point, the expanse of colors went on to the horizon.

“Do you like it?” Maggie asked as she took off her helmet and dismounted.

Preacher just sat there.

“Well, do ya?” she asked again.

“Be quiet,” Preacher said; “it’s too beautiful to spoil with words.”

Maggie nodded and smiled. She walked out on the vista and sat down, letting the soft breeze carry the smells of the desert to her nostrils. She breathed deep. When Preacher didn’t join her, she looked back to see him straddle his bike, smoking. She knew the peace of the desert. He was enjoying the experience.

She heard his boots on the gravel but didn't turn around. She waited for him to sit next to her.

"Maggie, this is every bit as good as the pond. This view is as good as it gets."

"I like it," she said.

"This reminds me of Dead Horse Point in southern Utah. You can see forever."

"I knew you'd like it. It's peaceful."

"That it is," he said.

They didn't talk for awhile. They only enjoyed the serenity of the place.

"Preacher, we have to get back. I only gave Mom a snack. I've got to go home and fix us supper."

"What are you cooking?" he asked.

"All you've eaten today is sandwiches. I thought that our last night alone should be something special. So, I took out some pork chops. How does pork chops with stuffing sound?"

"You mean stuffed pork chops?" he asked.

"No, I mean pork chops broiled with stuffing on the side."

"That'll work."

They climbed back on his bike and headed back to Hank's.

* * * * * * *

Hank and Tina awoke to a fresh Monday morning. Both had slept soundly. Roy, however, was not rested at all. After dinner at the smorgie, they had returned to the motel for a much needed rest. Tina had assigned one bed to herself and the other to the two men. The beds were queen sized, but that still didn't leave Roy with much room when Hank crawled in one side. Twice during the night, he had been startled awake when Hank's hand had landed across his shoulders. He finally resigned himself to the fact that if he was to get any sleep, he had to move. His first option was to crawl in the bed with Tina. After all, they were engaged. Realizing the prudence of that decision, he had pulled off the bed spread, grabbed a pillow, and curled up on the floor.

Tina had been the first to call attention to the fact that Roy hadn't gotten much sleep.

"Was the floor comfortable?" she asked. Roy grumbled; Hank laughed.

"You might practice that sleeping arrangement again," Hank said.

"Why would I want to practice sleeping on the floor?" Roy asked.

"Well," Hank said, "if you two are going to be married, you might find yourself sleeping there more often than you think."

Tina laughed and said, "Dad, I'll let him use the couch."

Roy commented on the arrangement. "I will not be the one sleeping on the couch; I'm sleeping in my own bed."

Hank replied, "We'll see." The camaraderie between them held as they showered and dressed. Now they were ready to greet the day.

"Should we eat first or go see Josh?" Hank asked.

"I want to go see Josh first," Tina said.

"I want to go back to sleep," Roy said.

"You can take a nap this afternoon. I want to see Josh first then we need to get him some clothes," Tina commented.

Hank put his hands in his pockets and looked at Roy. "Son, how much money do the two of you have?" he asked. He continued, "I'm down to about forty dollars. If I fill my truck up, I might have enough for a soda on my way home."

Tina intervened, "Dad, I have thirty dollars cash, but I brought my checkbook. I think we'll be okay."

"Roy?" Hank asked.

"Well, I have the ranch credit card for the motel, and forty-five dollars cash. I agree with Tina; I think we'll be okay."

"Okay," Hank said. "I think we should go check on Josh, and then I'll stay with him while you two go looking for clothes."

"How about some breakfast?" Roy asked.

"Tina," Hank said, "go next door and buy your man a doughnut or something. I don't want him complaining...not yet.

We have one more night to spend in this town, and then we'll go home. Josh will be active today. He'll be wanting to go home.

"Anything special you want to do today, Tina?" Roy asked.

"No, I think after we get Josh some clothes for tomorrow, I might let you take a nap while I call Maggie. "Dad," she asked, "if they let him go by ten in the morning, when do you think we'll be home, around two?"

Hank thought for a moment. "I'd say that works out right. We'll check out in the morning, get gas on our way out of town; yeah, I think two is a safe bet."

Josh was indeed awake and active when the trio arrived at the hospital. He was watching cartoons when they arrived.

"Good morning, son," Tina said. "How are you feeling this morning?"

"Good," he said, never taking his eyes off the TV.

"Did you have breakfast already?" she asked.

"Yup, fruit loops," he said.

Roy smiled, "Talkative this morning, aren't you?"

Josh looked at his soon-to-be dad and said, "Are we going home today?"

Roy shook his head and said, "I don't think so. The doctor wants to wait one more day. We'll see what he says when he gets here."

"He's here," came a voice from behind them. "And I'd say you'll be home by tomorrow afternoon. After looking at the charts and talking with your nurses, I think you can go home tomorrow. Does that sound okay to you, young man?" the doctor said.

"Yeah, I want to go home. Mom, are we still staying at the ranch?"

"Yes, son; we're moving out to the ranch."

"Good. I want to give that old ram a good kicking for hurting me."

Roy chimed in, "I don't think you'll be doing much of anything until that head and arm heal."

The doctor chuckled, "I think you'd better take it easy for awhile, Josh. No more riding sheep until that cast comes off."

"Okay," Josh said dejectedly as he turned back to his cartoons.

The doctor looked at Tina. "Ms. Kyle, can we step out in the hall for a moment?"

"Sure. Is there something wrong?"

"Not with this child, but I do have some concerns," he said as he led her out the door.

Roy looked over at Hank as Hank looked over at him. Hank nodded his head toward the door. Roy followed them out.

"Ms. Kyle, this sounds cold, but I noticed that you don't show an insurance carrier."

Tina looked at her hands. Roy spoke first.

"Doc, we don't have insurance. I don't know how much this whole thing is going to cost, but we'll pay it. You have my word."

The doctor smiled at the young couple. "I never had a doubt. The hospital will not carry the balance more than a month or so, and then they will help you make arrangements with a lending institution. I think you should talk to them sometime today. I'm going to release Josh tomorrow. It would be nice if this whole package could be wrapped up by then. Don't you think?"

Roy met the doctor's eyes with stoic eyes of his own. "Doc, you don't worry about a thing. We'll take care of it."

"Good; see you both in the morning."

After the doctor left, Tina looked up at Roy, "How are we going to pay it, Roy?"

"I don't know yet, but we will."

"Okay, if you say so, but I think we'd better look into health insurance pretty soon. With a son to raise, and maybe in time, a daughter, I don't think we can afford not to have it."

"We'll check into it as soon as we get home."

Hank stuck his head out the door. "Is everything okay?"

"Yes, Dad."

They walked back into Josh's room.

"Well, what did the doctor say?" Hank asked.

"You heard everything we did. Josh gets released in the morning. He suggested that we go talk to accounting. We need to see what arrangements we can make to pay for this little fiasco."

Hank grinned, "Well then, I'll leave you two to do what you have to do. I'm going back in with Josh and watch ninjas."

* * * * * * *

The ride back from the vista had been exhilarating. When they had reached the blacktop, Preacher had rolled back the throttle. They both liked the wind in their faces at eighty miles per hour. His black beauty had performed admirably. Back at the station, Preacher wiped his old girl down while Maggie took care of her mother and started dinner.

Tomorrow, if I get the chance, I'll check her over. She needs to be in top form if I'm going to get to Zion without a problem, he thought. He had adjusted his lifters last Friday, but it was a shovel with hydraulic lifters, so they probably needed it again. After putting his bike to bed, Preacher grabbed some clothes and headed over to Maggie's.

Preacher ambled through Maggie's back door to find her sitting on the arm of the couch with the telephone held to her ear. She looked up at him and silently mimicked "Tina." He nodded his head, rubbed his hand across her shoulder as he strolled into the bathroom and turned on the shower. He was shaving, wearing only his Levi's, when Maggie leaned on the door jam and folded her arms together across her chest, "Well, Preacher, the party's a go. I told Tina what we were doing for Josh. She thinks it's an excellent idea."

"Good," he replied.

"I told her about us too."

Preacher looked in the mirror to catch her eyes. "Us?" he asked.

"Yes. I told her we have been spending the evenings together."

"And?"

"She asked if I had slept with you yet."

"And?"

Maggie looked back at him in the mirror. With a rebellious tone she said, "I told her we were."

Preacher liked the look of challenge on her face. He smiled. "Well, there goes my reputation," he said as he resumed shaving.

As nonchalantly as she could, she continued, "I'm not ashamed to say that we're sleeping together. I told Gene this morning."

"I'll never live it down," he chided.

She smiled back at him through the mirror. "You're right; you won't. Now everybody will know that I've staked my claim."

Preacher wiped his face with a towel as he turned around to face her. "So, now I'm your property?"

"Yup. Every time you come through this town, everybody will say, there goes Maggie's ol' man. I like the sound of it."

"Well, if I'm your ol' man, that means you have to take care of me. I like the sound of that."

"You would," she said as she stood up straight. "I mean it, though. You only want to use my body."

In his finest brogue, he replied, "And a fine body it is, my lady."

"Don't you have even one romantic bone in your whole body?" she asked.

"Not the last time I looked, but I think that later we might find one."

Exasperated, Maggie sighed and said, "You *are* impossible, do you know that?"

"Yes, as a matter of fact, I do," he replied with a smile.

She shook her head. "Put a shirt on before dinner. I'll not have a man sitting at my table that isn't wearing a shirt."

"Yes, dear," was his reply.

Their dinner was excellent. Throughout the meal, they discussed the preparations necessary for the party. Preacher volunteered to barbecue the polish sausages. Maggie changed it from hot dogs to sausages. What kind of cake to serve? Carrot cake. Where to hang the banner? On the station. And the placing of the tables? Under the big cottonwood tree.

"Do you think I should make the cake tonight?" Maggie asked.

"It's up to you," Preacher said. "You're the chef."

She started scurrying around the small kitchen. "I think I will. Go smoke or something while I clean up this mess and start the cake."

"Okay," he said.

Maggie found him where she thought he would be: under the tree, on the bench, smoking. "You like it out here, don't you?" she asked as she sat down and pulled her legs up and off to the side.

"This is where it all began," he said. "The first night I spent in this place, I came out here to smoke. Hank caught me."

Maggie smiled, "He didn't say a word, did he?"

"Oh yeah, he told me it was against the law. He also said he didn't care what I did, as long as I didn't do it around Josh."

"He's a good man, Preacher. You're not the first wayfaring stranger he's helped."

"That's what I gathered. This station's the town's communication center."

"Yup, it is," Maggie said as she unfolded to stand up. "How long are you going to be?"

"I don't know, a minute or two, why?"

"I need to take the cake out. I'll see ya when you come in."

"Okay," he said as he rested his back against the tree. It is restful out here, he thought. He remembered his old house. He used to sit out on the veranda, with his feet up on the hand rail, and smoke. Now you're sitting on a bench around a big tree; he smiled at the thought. Maybe after I finish this road trip, I'll build another house, he thought, and get a dog. With a smile on his face he got up and ambled across the highway. He found Maggie in the kitchen, cleaning up. "Do you need some help?" he asked.

"Only if you want to dry some dishes," she replied as she looked up from a sink full of soapy water.

"I can do that," he said as he plucked a dish towel from the handle of the refrigerator and rolled it up. The towel cracked when it connected with her Levi-covered rear view.

Maggie spun around, "So, you want to play, huh?" She challenged with her right hand, still in the suds. "Okay...try this," she said as she threw a bowl full of soapy water in his face.

The fight was on. Preacher flipping his towel and Maggie with the spray nozzle. They ended up in a heap on the wet floor.

"A couple of those towel shots hurt," she said.

"Not to say anything about the soap in my eyes," Preacher responded as he sat up on the soaked floor and wiped his eyes.

"Do you want me to kiss them better?" she asked as she grabbed his shoulders and dragged him back down on the floor to join her. He took her with brutal abandon, missionary style.

Lying on the floor as they fought to regain their breath, Maggie looked over at Preacher and said, "I think I enjoyed that."

"You think," Preacher said.

"Yeah; between the welts from the towel, and the bruise I'm sure I'm going to have, I'll be sore in the morning."

"Well, if you're walking a little bowlegged tomorrow, everybody will know you've been laid; oh, I forgot, everybody does know."

She hit his shoulder, "Not everybody."

"Who doesn't know?" he asked.

"Hank," she said as she sat up.

"Does that bother you?" he asked.

"Maybe a little," she said. "He's been a father figure to me for a lot of years."

"Would you be embarrassed if he knew?" he asked.

"At first I would have been, but not now. At first you were just a traveler that interested me. All I wanted was some good, hot sex. That would have embarrassed me and Hank. Now, I want the whole town to know. You *are* the man Maggie gives her body to. Every time anybody thinks of this accident, they will think about us. I can live with the idea of being your woman. It gives us history. Can you understand that?"

"Maggie," Preacher said in a warning voice.

"I know, you're leaving. If I was living with you, you'd still leave. You'll always be leaving for this reason or that. Sometimes I could go; sometimes I'd have to stay home. I know that. I'm going to deal with your leaving with that in mind. Sometimes you leave alone. Sometimes I can go with you. This time I stay behind.

"And if I don't come back?" he asked.

"You'll come back," she said.

"Ya think? What makes you so sure?"

"Once you've had the best, the rest is a waste of time," she said with a smile, "and Preacher, you've had the best. Now, let's clean up this mess." She stood and offered a hand to Preacher, "Come on, let's get busy. The mop and pail are out by the washer."

* * * * * * *

Maggie woke to the even breathing of Preacher. She knew he was still asleep. She smiled with the memory of their juvenile behavior the evening prior. With that memory, came the reminder of the towel, and the sex.

She moved her legs—yup, a little stiff. He had let himself go. Last night he had taken her for his own use. It had been exhilarating. Together they had mopped the floor, put on dry comfortable clothes and had put the wet ones in the dryer. He had watched TV while she finished the cake. Both of them had been comfortable with the scenario. Today, however, was going to be a busy one. She had to get up and get the diner open. Preacher had to set up for the party and run the station.

She shook his shoulder. "Preacher, are you awake?"

"I am now," he muttered. "Go away; I need my rest."

"You can rest on your own time. Come on, wake up. We've got a lot to do today."

"Then get up and start doing. I don't have to get up until six. It's, what, four-thirty now?"

"It's more like twenty till five. Come on, wake up."

"You go shower, and then I'll get up," he said.

"No, you get up and start the coffee while I shower and dress. Come on, get up. I need your help today."

"What do you want me to do, make the biscuits or heat up the gravy?" he asked.

"I need your help with the macaroni salad."

"Do I get to make it my way?"

"And what way is that?" she asked.

"With sweet pickle relish," he said.

Maggie shook her head and said with a smile, "You and your sweet tooth. Alright, do it your way."

"Good," he said as he sat up.

Maggie crawled out of bed and gingerly walked into the bathroom.

Preacher smiled, "A little sore this morning?" he asked.

"I told you I probably would be. You all but raped me last night," she called as he heard her turn on the shower.

"I couldn't control myself." He heard her laugh as she got into the shower. He pulled on some Levi's and headed for the kitchen.

Preacher was leaning against the counter with a cup of coffee in his hand when Maggie walked into her small kitchen. She was fussing with her bun when she walked through the door.

"The transition is complete," he said as she walked in.

"What do you mean by that?" she asked.

"You're like a chameleon. You change to fit the surroundings."

"I do not," she said as she poured herself a cup of the aromatic brew.

"Bullshit; last night you were a different person than you will be in the diner."

"I have to work, Preacher. That doesn't mean I'm not the same. It means that I have to put on my uniform and go to work."

"I understand having to work, and I understand the uniform, but you act differently when you're in the diner. You don't have water fights in the diner."

"And we're not going to have one in there today, either. I have a lot to do today and so do you. So behave yourself," she admonished.

"I never get to have any fun," he whined.

"You had enough fun last night. Now, come on, get dressed. I'll see you in the other kitchen," she said as she walked purposely out of the kitchen. He heard the front door close.

Maggie was, again, making biscuits when Preacher walked into the "other" kitchen.

"I think I've been here before," he said as he sauntered past the counter into the kitchen.

"Yes, you have," Maggie replied as she worked the large mound of dough. "Preacher, would you put that cake in the big fridge over there?" she pointed with her chin.

"Sure, anything else?" he asked.

"Yes, grab that big pot and fill it with water."

Preacher smiled to himself. She's got a party to put together. She's on a mission, he thought.

"Okay," he said as he put his coffee cup down.

"Preacher, the tables are out in the garage next to the Malibu, when you're finished in here."

"Whoa, girl, who made you boss today?" he asked as he put the big pot in the sink.

Exasperated, Maggie said, "We have a lot to do today, Preacher. We've got to get busy."

In a stern voice he said, "I know what I have to do today. I don't need you driving me."

"You needed to know where the tables were," she said as she kneaded the dough.

"Maggie," Preacher said.

She looked up from the dough. "Okay, I'm sorry. You know what you need to do, and I know what I need to do. If you can't find what you need, please ask, okay?"

With a smirk on his face, he replied, "That works for me."

"I'm glad that works for you," she said. "Now, will you please fill that pan with water and put it on the stove?" she asked with a smirk.

"Anything to please the lady," he replied.

"Jerk," she said.

"I resemble that," he replied as he turned the water on to fill the pot.

It was going to be a good day.

Preacher was leaning against the work table, eating macaroni salad with sweet pickle relish when Maggie looked up from the biscuits, fresh from the stove, and said, "Preacher, would you please open the front door, it's six o'clock. Charlie and Frank are probably outside already."

"Sure," he said as he stood and put his salad down. "Are you sure you want me to open the front door? What will the neighbors think?"

She looked up from the biscuits, "Please," she replied.

"Okay." As he walked up to the door, Preacher noticed a truck out front. Yup, it's Charlie and Frank. He opened the door.

"Morning," Preacher said as they opened their doors and stepped down.

"Morning," Frank said as he stepped up on the porch. "Getting an early start, are ya?" he asked.

With a gleam in his eye, Preacher looked at Frank and said, "You know Maggie. She has a party to put together. She's already got me working."

Frank smiled at Preacher and responded, "It's good to get your chores done early if it makes the old woman happy."

Preacher nodded his head, "And, Maggie is not a woman I would want mad at me."

Frank nodded and said, "Me neither."

Charlie looked over at Frank, "But, he doesn't open the station until eight. He doesn't have any chores."

Frank looked back at Preacher. "Charlie, any time you're involved with a woman, you have chores."

Charlie was muttering as they walked through the door and took their places at the counter.

"Good morning," Maggie said as she set up their coffee cups. "How are you two this morning?"

"Fine," Frank said. "I hear you've already got Preacher working."

"The kids are coming home today. We're having a coming home party for Josh. You knew that, didn't you?"

"Gene did say there was going to be a get together this afternoon. I told my wife, and she's making a cobbler."

Maggie nodded, "I've got the cake made." She looked at Preacher, "Preacher made *his* macaroni salad, and he's offered to barbecue over under the tree. The kids will be here around two, so be back before then, okay?"

"Sure, I can do that. Charlie, what do you have to do this morning?"

It didn't take long for the diner to start filling up with neighbors.

Preacher picked up his coffee cup and watched with a smile as the community came together for Josh's party.

Preacher walked over to the station a little after seven. He greeted the rabbits prior to stepping in the back door. He flipped on the bay lights and his bedroom light. He had brought over his laundry. Now would be a good time to pack and get ready for tomorrow. He rolled his Levi's, socks, and T-shirts and set them on his bed. He would pack his saddle bags tonight. This was the perfect time to check his old girl over. He found his trusty old milk crate and sat down. He popped the covers off the pushrods and began adjusting the lifters. He had barely snapped the last cover on when Gene walked in the front door.

"Getting ready to leave?" he asked.

"I thought I might as well check her over this morning. Maggie will have me running before too long. I probably won't have a chance once we start setting up."

"Where are you setting up?" he asked.

"I think you'd better go over to *Maggie's*. The folks over there are figuring that out right now," Preacher replied as he wiped the pushrod covers.

"Alright, I will. Do you want anything from over there?" Gene asked.

"Naw, I'll be fine. Thanks," he replied.

Gene ambled over to *Maggie's*.

"Good morning, Gene," Maggie said as he stepped through the front door.

"Good morning, Maggie." He continued, "I just talked to Preacher, and he said you were running the show today."

"What's he doing?" she asked.

"Getting ready to leave."

Startled, Maggie looked up from pouring coffee. "Leave? He's not supposed to leave until tomorrow."

"He's not. He's just getting ready."

The diner was quiet as they all looked at her and awaited her response. "Well, he said he was leaving when Hank came home, and Hank's coming home today." She paused. "Okay, he's leaving," she said matter-of-factly. "Gene, when are you and your wife coming into town?" she asked.

"Around one. That way the missus can set up her things before the kids show up."

"What's she bringing?" she asked.

The diner erupted when everybody started talking about who was bringing what and when.

Preacher finished wiping his old girl down. He checked his oil and pushed his beast out to top off the tanks. Then he pushed his bike back into the first bay and grabbed the hose.

I'd better wash up around the pumps and let it dry before we get carried away, he thought. He was spraying the approaches to the pumps when Charlie and Frank walked out of *Maggie's*.

Frank hollered over, "Still doing chores?"

Preacher looked up and nodded his head yes.

Charlie looked at Frank and said, "Hank's never had the place cleaned up like this."

"I know," Frank replied as they got into the truck and left.

Gene was next to leave *Maggie's*. He walked over to his truck under the tree. "Preacher, I'll bring in a couple more tables when I get back. If everybody brings what they're saying, we'll need them."

"Okay. I'll get the ones Maggie has set up around noon."

"Alright," Gene said. "I'll be back by one. See you then, and thanks."

"Thanks for what?" Preacher asked.

"All you've done," Gene replied.

"Not a problem," he replied.

"Hank's going to be lost in this place after you're gone." Gene chuckled. "He won't be able to find anything."

Preacher chuckled, "Serves him right. Him gallivanting down in Reno and leaving me here to do all his work, it doesn't seem fair."

Gene was smiling when he left in his truck.

The sound brought Preacher's head up. He had been raking the gravel around the tree when the sound of a motorcycle caught his attention. He stood up. It coughed and sputtered its way up to the pumps. The bike was a mess. It was an old Sportster, and it had seen its better days. The handle bars were bent, the gas tank was dented, the seat was torn, the back tire was bald, and it was filthy. The rider pulled off his full helmet. It was Eddie. Preacher leaned his rake against the bench and started walking toward him.

"Give me some gas!" Eddie demanded.

"No, I don't think I'll do that," Preacher said in a mild tone.

Eddie responded with a belligerent tone, "Who in the fuck are you to tell me 'no'. I said, give me some gas!"

Eddie's head rocked back, and his knees buckled when Preacher's straight right hand collided with his chin. He fell to his knees. Preacher bent down and grabbed a handful of his greasy hair and pulled his head back. "I said no," Preacher said. He put his boot on Eddie's chest and pushed him over. "Now get on that thing and leave before you hurt yourself."

Eddie started to get up when he said, "I'll get you for that, asshole."

Preacher knocked him down again. "You do that," he said in his mild tone.

Eddie was glaring at Preacher when he got up. He didn't say a word when he started the wreck and chugged off.

* * * * * * *

Maggie looked out the front windows when she heard Eddie's bike. "Oh my God," she said.

John was sitting at the counter eating his breakfast when he overheard Maggie.

"What did you say?" he asked.

"Eddie's over at Hank's," she said in an anxious tone.

"This I want to see," John said as he jumped up and ran for the window. When Preacher knocked Eddie down the first time, John said, "Yes."

Maggie stepped out on the porch as Eddie was leaving. She smiled and asked with arrogance, "Preacher, do you have a problem?"

Preacher waved at Maggie and smiled, "Other than needing a little Raid for the cockroaches, everything is just fine."

She walked over to him. "How's your hand?" she asked as she ambled up to him.

"Fine. It would take more than that piece of shit to hurt my hand," he said.

Maggie looked up at him, "He'll be back, Preacher."

He smiled and said, "Okay. I could use the workout. Lounging around here and eating your cooking, I've added a few pounds."

She shook her head. "He won't come back alone."

Preacher put his arm around her shoulders and started her across the street toward the diner. "Thanks for the warning. I'll try to be prepared."

Maggie stepped up on the porch. "You're something, Preacher. I'm beginning to think you enjoyed it."

"It wasn't so bad. He ran into my fist. I didn't do anything."

"Preacher, I watched out the window."

"Then you know I'm innocent."

Maggie framed his face with her hands. "You're about as innocent as a stick of dynamite with a short fuse."

"Are you saying my fuse is too short? Why, I thought it suited you just fine."

"That fuse I like; the other one could use some work."

"He was disrespectful, Maggie."

"I know, I know. Just try not to get into any more fights this afternoon, okay?"

"If he comes back, Maggie, I'll have to meet his challenge. You know that."

"Yeah, I know that. Do what you think is right." She smiled at him, "Far be it from me to tell *you* what to do."

"Now you're learning," he responded. He swatted her butt when she turned to go back into the diner.

She spun around and asked, "What did you do that for?"

He smiled, "Cause I can."

"Go back to work; you're having way too much fun." She was smiling when she walked back into the diner.

John was waiting when Maggie sauntered in the front door. "What happened? Why did he hit Eddie?" he asked.

Maggie looked back to see Preacher walking back to the tree and rake. "You may not understand this, John, but Eddie was disrespectful."

"Preacher hit him cause he was disrespectful? That doesn't seem right to me. If Eddie had hit him first, I could see it, but because he was disrespectful?"

Maggie patted John's shoulder. "I told you, you wouldn't understand. By his rules, respect is the one thing he insists on. He will fight for it. He doesn't care if you like him or not, but you'd better be respectful, or he will discipline you."

John shook his head. With a look of confusion, he asked, "Is he really that mean?"

Maggie laughed, "He's not mean. Look what he's done for Hank and the kids. It's his code, John. That's how he lives."

John sat down at the counter. "I think I'll just be quiet when he's around. It's safer."

Now Maggie did laugh. John would never understand the biker's code. Brothers of the road know the code. Merely owning a motorcycle doesn't make you a biker. You have to earn respect. You have to learn the code. You have to ride. On the road, it's not the colors, it's the code.

Maggie had lived with a biker. She knew the code. She knew Preacher was a good man. Society would never understand him. It had only one code: money.

She was still smiling as she walked back into the kitchen. She had a lot to do before the kids came home.

* * * * * * *

Tina was bustling around the motel room. "Roy, would you please hand me that uniform? I need to pack it," she said. "Dad, do you have everything out of here?"

"It's all in the truck except this sack," he replied.

"Good," she said. "It's ten o'clock, and Josh will be released at eleven. We need to hurry."

The trio had awoke in good spirits. Today they were all going home. The last couple of days had not been as stressful as the first few had been. Josh had recovered to the point of getting bored. They had talked to the financial group at the hospital and had been assured that they would be in touch. All that was left to do was pack, get Josh, and go home.

"Tina, are you going to ride with me or your dad?"

"I think I'll leave that decision up to Josh. Whatever he wants is okay with me."

"So, you're riding with Josh?"

"Of course," she said.

Roy studied Tina for a moment, "I thought the three of us could ride together. Hank, would you have a problem with driving back home alone?"

Hank looked at Tina then back at Roy, "Son, if you want to take your bride to be and your son home, that's fine with me. If I left now, I could stop by Fallon and pick up something I've been thinking about."

"What's that?" Tina asked.

Hank grinned at Tina, "I want to get Preacher and Maggie a little something for helping us. That's all."

"Well, if you really don't mind," Tina said as she looked at Roy.

"Go ahead, Hank," Roy said. "I'll bring the family home."

"Good," Hank said. "Tina, give me some of your money, and I'll leave as soon as we're checked out."

Tina picked up her purse. "How much do you need?"

Hank replied, "Whatever cash you have. Roy has enough to get you home, and you have your checkbook. That'll be enough."

"What are you going to buy for Maggie?" Tina asked.

"I thought flowers," Hank said.

Tina handed Hank her thirty-five dollars. "Make it a spring bouquet. That way she can put it by the cash register."

"Okay, spring flowers it is."

Tina looked at her father. "Dad, thanks for being here for us."

"No problem. That's what families are for."

"Thanks, Hank," Roy said as he extended his hand.

Hank shook it. "Take care on the way home, son."

"I will."

Hank picked up his sack of odds and ends, along with all the leftover soap and shampoo that the motel had supplied, and headed out to his truck.

Tina looked at Roy.

"Do you think he knows Maggie and Preacher have been seeing each other?" she asked.

"No," Roy said. "Maggie won't date anybody, let alone see some stranger. I don't think your dad has even thought about it."

"Then he's in for a big surprise. I'll bet the whole town knows," Tina stated.

"That wouldn't surprise me none. Charlie can't keep a secret worth a damn."

The morning was alive with birds as they walked out to the trucks. Tina stopped at her dad's truck. "Dad, you be careful on the way home."

"I will."

Tina kissed his grizzled cheek. "We'll be about an hour behind you. If anything happens, just sit there and we'll be by."

"Don't you worry about me, Tina. You two just get yourselves home safe. I'll be fine."

"Alright," she said, "we'll see ya at home."

"See ya later," Hank said as he crawled into his truck.

Josh was waiting when they sauntered into his room. The sight of Josh with his bright white cast and his shaved head with its bandage, made Tina smile. His eyes were bright, and he wore a smile.

"Good morning, Josh."

"Hi, Mom."

"Are you ready to go home?"

"Yup. I can't wait till I can see that ram again."

Roy smiled, "Why do you want to see that old ram again? You can't ride him."

"I don't want to ride him; I want to eat him."

Tina and Roy laughed. Roy asked, "You want to eat him?"

"Yeah, Maggie makes the best stew, and I want him in the pot."

They both erupted with laughter. Still smiling, Tina said, "We'll talk about the ram later. You need to get dressed and get ready. Grandpa has already gone home."

"Okay," Josh said as he climbed out of his hospital bed.

After leaving the hospital, Josh was in good spirits. His incessant chatter was nonstop for the first half hour. Tina and Roy endured it stoically. After they passed through the town of Sparks, Josh complained that his arm was hurting, and Tina gave him one pain pill. Now he was stretched out on the seat with his head on his mother's lap and his feet on Roy's, asleep. Tina didn't remember a lot about the drive to Reno. She had been too busy cussing Roy to notice. Now, however, she did notice.

As they turned onto Highway 50, she began to notice that the lupine had dropped most of its flowers. They had begun to develop the tiny pods that all legumes had in common. The goldenrod still had their flowers, but they were covered with dust. She liked this country, with all its yews of different colors and shapes. And, she was getting married. She looked over at Roy and smiled. He will be a good father, she thought.

* * * * * * *

The bout with Eddie had left Preacher in a good mood. Eddie was a bully. He picked on the ones he could intimidate. Preacher was not impressed. Bullies are always afraid. They are afraid that if they can't control a person, they won't be respected. Control is the issue, not respect. Preacher smiled the entire time he was raking rocks around the tree.

Next on his list was the banner. Preacher walked through the front door of the diner and into the kitchen. "Maggie, where do you keep the butcher paper? I need to make the banner."

The diner was all but empty. Two travelers sat at the counter, finishing breakfast. Maggie, however, was busy.

"It's under that counter over there," she pointed toward the serving station.

"And Magic Markers?" he asked.

"Under the cash register."

"Thanks," he said as he left with the paper and markers.

He rolled out the paper on the workbench. Next, he blocked in the letters with a pencil and then retraced them with the black marker. It read "Welcome Home, Josh".

Once the letters were filled in, he added some art work of his own. Harley-Davidson wings complemented the two top outside corners. A black sheep with huge curling horns, facing a boy with a bandage on his head, adorned the bottom of the banner. With some tape left over from the painting, he attached the banner to the second bay door. The tables were next. He found them where Maggie had said they would be. He hauled them over to the tree and set them up. After wiping them down, he covered them with the white paper. He found a big black kettle barbecue outside of Maggie's garage. He placed it in the shade of the tree along with the tables. He stood back and looked at the setup. Something was missing. The setting didn't balance. He began smiling after a moment of thought. Walking into the first bay, he stopped and looked at his old girl. This will do nicely, he thought. He pushed the gleaming black beast out into the sun in front of the first bay. He didn't hear Maggie as she strolled up behind him.

"You look awful satisfied with yourself," she said.

"I am," he countered.

"All we need now is a party," she said.

"That'll come soon enough," he replied.

"Are you going to want some lunch?" she asked.

"I don't think so. Once all the food arrives, I don't think any of us will be hungry."

"Well, it's almost one. Everybody should start showing up any time now."

He turned and looked at her, "How do you want to do this? If the kids don't arrive until two, when do you want to put the food out?"

"As it comes in, I guess. It should be okay, as long as it's in the shade."

"Gene told me he would bring in a couple of tables. I'll set them up and cover them then you can do your thing with the locals."

"The locals?" she asked.

"Yeah, the locals. I know a few, like Gene and Frank, but most of them are your friends, not mine."

"They all know what you've done for Hank. Some are even anxious to meet you. The least you could do is be friendly."

"I'll be cooking sausages, so I guess I'll have to meet them all."

"Probably, so be nice."

"I'm always nice," he countered.

"Yeah, right. I'll go close up and then change. I'll be back in a minute," she said as she headed back to the diner.

"Okay," he said as he surveyed the station again.

Preacher strolled back to his bedroom. It was time to medicate. If I have to put up with these people, I might as well enjoy it, he thought. He picked up his saddle bags.

Maggie found him leaning against the door jam of the back door smoking.

"A little attitude adjustment?" she asked as she wrapped her arms around his waist from behind.

"You never know when you're going to need an attitude," he replied as he reached around and encircled her shoulders with his arm and pulled her to his side.

"Preacher, I want to thank you for all that you've done for us."

"Not a problem. You can thank me later."

"And I will!" She paused. "The kids are coming home and you're leaving. I don't know if I should be happy or sad."

"Take one day at a time, Maggie. Control what you can control, and to hell with the rest. You can't control it anyway."

"Well, I don't seem to have any control over you," she said.

"And you never will. I'm like the eagle. If you cage me, I'll get mean or die, but if you turn me loose, I might just come back for a visit once in a while."

She looked up at him, "And I'll always feed you."

Preacher smiled. "Now that's a good woman," he said.

She swatted his butt, "Then take this good woman out front and let's get ready for the party." She disengaged and turned toward the front of the station. Maggie had changed out of her uniform. She now wore bright blue Levi's with a tooled belt and buckle, a sleeveless white blouse, tucked in, and her moccasins.

She had brushed out her long thick red hair. It surrounded her head and shoulders like a shawl.

Preacher slipped into his room and changed his T-shirt. He now donned a sleeveless black UBNC T-shirt and his scrodie. As he ambled out of the bay, he noticed that both Gene and Miguel had pulled up to the tree and parked. Gene's truck had two folding tables in the back; Miguel's was stacked with folding chairs.

"Preacher!" Gene called. "Where do you want this stuff?"

"Ask Maggie. I told you once before that I'm not the boss. This affair is yours, not mine. I'm only here to cook."

Gene smiled and strolled over to shake Preacher's hand. "Thanks for all you've done, Preacher."

"Not a problem," he said.

Gene looked around. "What do you say to putting the chairs in the shade for the women, and we could add the tables to the row you've already started."

"Let's get to it," Preacher said as he started toward the trucks.

Maggie, Lupe, and Gene's wife were hauling food out of the trucks.

It didn't take long until the side of the station was a parking lot. Frank and his wife along with Charlie and his wife had shown up.

John had come alone, but his wife had sent a dish.

"Preacher," Maggie called, "would you go get the macaroni salad please?"

Preacher was still setting up chairs when she called. He held up his index finger to let her know he had heard and would do it in a minute.

Gene looked over at Preacher. "Your lady calls," he said.

"She's been calling all day. She can wait for a minute."

"Never keep a woman waiting, Preacher."

Preacher stood up and looked over at Maggie then back at Gene. "Whatever you say, boss."

Gene's face bloomed when a big grin crossed his face. "Then do as you're told, Preacher."

"*Asked*, Gene, *asked*," he responded.

"Okay, *asked*," Gene said. Gene just shook his head as Preacher wandered over to the diner.

Preacher came back with the salad and handed it to Maggie. "When do you want the cake?" he asked.

"Later, after we've eaten," she said as she took the bowl of salad.

The tables were all but covered with the various dishes that the women had brought. Potato salad, macaroni salad, and Jell-O salad were in one group. Baked beans and scalloped potatoes were next in line, with desserts on the end. Lupe had made Mexican bread.

Maggie walked up to Preacher and took a hold of his scrodie near the bottom. "Is it time to start the briquettes yet?" she asked.

"Probably, they take twenty minutes to get ready, but the sausages won't take too long to cook." He looked around at the group. He draped his arms on her shoulders and said, "I hope we bought enough."

"I think we'll be just fine. I ordered a hundred. What we don't use, I'll feed to them for a special."

"That works." He paused and looked down at her. "You've done well, Maggie, but there's one thing missing."

Maggie stood a little straighter. "What's that?" she asked.

"The donation jar," Preacher smiled.

Maggie asked, "Baby, would you go get it for me? It's on the counter."

"Sure," he replied, "be right back."

Everybody got excited when Preacher returned with the gallon jar full of money.

Charlie asked, "Maggie, how much is in there?"

Maggie put her hand on his shoulder and replied, "I don't know, Charlie. I emptied it once, but I haven't counted it."

"Guess," he said.

Preacher, overhearing the conversation, stepped over and said, "Maggie, we should have a contest to see who guesses closest."

Maggie smiled, “What’s the prize?”

Preacher reached into his Levi’s and withdrew a twenty dollar bill. “This,” he said as he held it up.

Maggie and Charlie beamed.

“Okay,” she said. She raised her hands and hollered, “Everybody, can I have your attention!” She paused. “Preacher is offering twenty dollars to the person who can come the closest to guessing the amount of money that’s in this jar.” She held it up. “This is most of the donations we have all made to Hank, Tina, and Roy. One dollar per pick. Winner takes all.”

Charlie grinned, “I’ll take one!” he yelled.

“Me too,” said Frank.

It didn’t take long until everybody had their dollar out and was eyeballing the jar.

Preacher walked back into the station and came out with paper and pen. Maggie started the list.

“Who’s going to count it?” Charlie asked.

Preacher looked over at him. “You are, Charlie. Make yourself useful.”

Charlie beamed. “Okay,” he said.

Preacher handed him the jar.

Maggie walked over to Preacher as he was lighting the briquettes. “We just made thirty more dollars. With the work you’ve done for Hank, you have been responsible for raising over five hundred dollars.”

“It’s for a good cause,” he said.

She looked at him for a moment. “Preacher, you ought to be proud of all that you’ve done for the kids, but this is only a drop in the bucket compared to their hospital bill.”

He looked up from the barbecue. “You do what you can and hope it turns out for the best. Like I said, control what you can.”

Maggie finished the saying, “And to hell with the rest, you can’t control it anyway.”

Preacher smiled, “You’re learning.”

“I’ve learned a lot from you, Preacher.”

He grinned, “Anything else you want to learn, just look me up.”

Now Maggie grinned. "I'll let you teach me tonight," she said.
Frank walked over. "Who's teaching whom?" he said with a smile.
"I'm learning," said Preacher.
"And what are you learning, Preacher?" Frank asked, still grinning.
"To do my chores before the little lady asks me to," he replied.
Frank nodded his head. "Maggie, you're doing a good job on this man. Keep it up. You might make him a citizen yet."
Maggie put her arm around his waist. "I don't want a citizen, Frank. I like him just the way he is."
Frank shook his head. As he walked off, he said, "Now the boys around here will *never* have a chance, not now that she's got him."
Maggie and Preacher both laughed.

* * * * * * *

Hank was the first one to show up at the station. As he was driving up to the station he slowed down. The sight of all the vehicles around the old cottonwood tree caused him some concern until he saw Preacher barbecuing. They were having a party. When he pulled up to the station it took his breath. The station was gleaming white. The pump base and the tower for the water and air was glowing red. He noticed the banner and immediately smiled. They were throwing a party for Josh.
Everybody stood up and looked at Hank. He opened the door of his truck and stepped down. Gene and Maggie walked up to the truck. Both were smiling. Gene offered Hank his hand. "Welcome back," he said.
"It's good to be back. What have you done to my station?" he asked as he turned and looked at the station again.
"We cleaned it up," Gene said.
"Maybe I didn't want it cleaned up," Hank said.
Maggie chimed in, "Too bad. You left Preacher to take care of it, and he got bored. So, this is your punishment."

Hank hugged Maggie. "Some punishment. Where is that jackass anyway?"

Gene answered, "He's cooking. I *know* he'll be happy to see ya."

Hank started over to Preacher. He didn't make it. Everybody wanted to hear about Josh and the trip.

Preacher smiled when he heard Hank call him a jackass. He enjoyed being a part of the homecoming. It never ceased to amaze him that people didn't come together unless there was a crisis. Why don't they do it for fun, was a question that he could never get answered. They were always busy. "I don't have time" was the standard response.

Hank finally made it over to Preacher. He stuck his hands in his pockets and asked, "How are you holding out, Preacher?"

"I thought I was a jackass," Preacher said with a smile.

"You are. What have you done to my station?" Hank asked.

"You leave me here with a crazy redhead and you ask *me* what I did to your station?"

"Has it been that hard on you?" Hank asked with some concern.

"No, Maggie and I have been getting along just fine. I still might marry her. That woman can cook."

"I told ya," Hank said with a smile.

"Where are the kids?" Preacher asked.

"They're right behind me, I think."

"I'll hold off putting the sausages on until they get here."

Maggie disentangled herself from the group of women and strolled up to Preacher and Hank. "So, have you two settled your differences yet?"

"What differences?" Hank asked.

"He's been complaining about being bored, and you've been complaining because he cleaned up your station."

Hank looked over at the station. "Where did you get the paint?" He looked back at Preacher.

"Gene brought it in."

Hank asked, "And you painted?"

"No, I hate to paint. Gene, Frank, and the rest of your old boys painted it."

"What were you doing?"

Preacher smiled and draped his hand over Maggie's shoulders. "We went on a picnic."

"A picnic?" Hank asked.

"Yup, fried chicken and the works."

"Fried chicken?" Hank asked again.

Maggie beamed as she said, "Yup, fried chicken and potato salad. Both of your favorites, Hank."

"And you didn't invite me?" he asked with a big smile on his face.

"Nope." Maggie squared her shoulders and put her arm around Preacher's waist. "We had the pond all to ourselves."

Hank looked at the pair. He liked what he saw. He looked up at Preacher. "You mean to tell me you took over my station and took my best girlfriend? It seems to me you can't be trusted, Preacher. After everything I've done for you, and you take my best girl. Well, I'll be damned."

Preacher was smiling, "That'll teach ya to leave me in charge. I'll make my own rules."

The sound of Roy's truck had everybody turning to watch as they arrived.

Hank looked back at Maggie. "Did Tina say anything about her and Roy?"

Maggie nodded, yes.

Hank asked, "Does anyone else know?"

"I don't know," Maggie said. "I told Preacher the other night, but I haven't said anything to anyone else."

Hank looked at the two of them, "I think I'll be wanting to know what else happened between you two. It seems like I can't leave either one of you alone."

Roy got out and walked around to open Tina's door. Everybody started toward the truck.

Gene was the first to engage his son. "How you doing, son?" he asked as the pair shook hands.

"Good, Dad. I hope everything went well at the ranch."

"It did. Your mother was a little worried though."

"I'm sorry I left like I did, but I felt I had to," Roy said.

"It's okay, Roy. Now that you're going to be his dad, you need to take care of your son."

"Thanks, Dad." They embraced.

"Now let me see the bride to be."

Tina blushed, "Hello, Gene."

"Welcome home," Gene said as he hugged her. He looked in the cab at Josh. "And how's my little bronc rider?"

Josh beamed, "Can I call you Grandpa now? We're going to be living at Roy's house, ya know."

Gene smiled, "Yes, I know, and yes, you can call me Grandpa."

Gene turned around to the group. "Ladies and gentlemen, I have an announcement to make."

The crowd quieted.

"Tina and Roy want to announce their upcoming marriage."

The group erupted with applause.

Hank looked back at Maggie. "It's about time," he said.

Maggie nodded her head yes.

"One hundred thirty-seven dollars and forty-five cents," Charlie chimed in.

Frank looked over at Charlie. "Then give me my twenty bucks. I picked one thirty-five."

Everybody laughed. Hank looked bewildered. "What was that all about?" he asked.

Maggie laughed, "It's how much was in the donation jar."

"What donation jar?" he asked.

"The one Preacher started the day after you left," she replied.

Hank looked over at Preacher. "You have been busy, haven't you?"

Preacher just smiled.

Maggie swatted Preacher's butt. "Start cooking, Preacher; we have a party to put on."

Preacher cooked; Maggie was the hostess. Everybody signed Josh's cast. Everybody congratulated Tina and Roy, and everybody ate. Josh was a little tired about midway through the party, so Tina escorted him over to Hank's house to rest.

Most of the men were huddled around the tree. Most of the women were grouped around Roy's mom and Lupe.

Tina came back out of the house and wandered over to join Preacher and Maggie at the barbecue. "Maggie, thanks for everything. It was good to have all our friends and family here to welcome us home. These last couple of days have been hectic."

Maggie replied, "You just be ready to work tomorrow."

Tina smiled, "I will. Now Preacher, I understand you and Miss Maggie have become friends. Is that right?"

Preacher draped his arm across Maggie's shoulders. "I don't know about friends, but she's definitely kept me busy."

Maggie slipped her arm around his waist and put her other hand on his stomach. "He's picked on. Can't you tell?" she said.

Tina smiled, "He looks picked on."

The trio laughed at their private joke.

A sound that all of them recognized had the whole group looking east, dreadfully. In a cloud of dust, a beat-up old truck slid to a stop. It was Eddie, and he was drunk. There was another man in the passenger seat. He was older than Eddie and just as slovenly. Eddie crawled out of the truck. He slurred, "I haven't missed the party, have I? Where is the rug rat anyway? I wanted to give him a hug."

Maggie tightened her grip on Preacher when he started forward. "Preacher, let it be."

"I don't think so," he said as he tried to untangle himself from Maggie.

Eddie looked over at the movement and noticed Preacher. "Ah, the biker trash and his bitches. Are you fucking them both, mister trash? How would you girls like to try a real man?"

Preacher started toward him.

"Damn it, Preacher," Maggie said as she stomped her foot.

The boys were all on their feet watching.

The older man walked up to Eddie's side.

Tina looked over at Maggie. "He'll get hurt, Maggie. There are two of them."

Maggie shook her head. "He'll do the hurting," she replied. "I just don't want him hurting himself."

They looked back toward the pending confrontation.

"Eddie, you're not welcome here," Roy said as he walked over from the tree. "I suggest you crawl back in that truck and leave."

Eddie looked over at Roy and grinned. "So the little bull has finally gotten some balls, huh?"

Roy kept walking.

Preacher got as far as the tables when Gene stopped him with a hand. "Hold on, Preacher," he said. "Let us deal with our own."

Preacher looked at Gene. "He's mine," Preacher said as he started forward.

Roy stopped in front of Eddie.

"Are you going to make me leave?" Eddie asked.

"If I have to," Roy replied.

"Then try," Eddie said as he threw a looping round house punch.

A lifetime of working on the ranch, building fences, and working with cattle and sheep, had honed Roy to the perfect balance between muscle and sinew. His left hand streaked through the space between them like a lightning bolt. With an audible crunch, Roy's fist connected with Eddie's nose. Roy stooped down. Two quick right hooks to the solar plexus and Eddie was standing on his toes. Roy had taken away his air. Eddie couldn't breathe. One quick left hook to the liver, and Eddie was leaning. A stinging right uppercut collided with the point of Eddie's chin. Eddie's teeth crashed together, his eyes rolled back, and he collapsed into a heap at Roy's feet.

"Why, you little bastard," the older man roared as he started to rush forward. Gene blocked his way. "I don't think you want to go there, Clem," Gene said. "I whipped you as a kid, and I'll whip you now."

The old man stopped.

Gene continued as he walked up to Roy's side, "Now gather up your son and go home. You're not welcome here anymore."

The old man was bewildered. Eddie groaned. The old man looked down. Eddie was throwing up.

"Pick him up and leave, Clem," Gene said in a warning tone.

The old man looked up at Gene. "He was drunk. I tried to stop him, but he wouldn't listen. He didn't mean it."

"Clem," Gene warned.

"Alright, alright, we're leaving," the old man said as he bent down and helped Eddie to his feet.

"Roy, if you broke your hand, I'm going to kill you," Tina said as she marched toward him.

Hank laughed, "Remember the floor, Roy?"

Roy grinned, "I didn't break anything but Eddie's nose, Tina, and yes I do remember the floor," he said to Hank.

Maggie sauntered up to Preacher, "That's been a long time coming."

Preacher smiled down at Maggie. "Remind me not to get in the way of that left hand. That guy could hurt a man."

Maggie stood at Preacher's side. She looped her arm around his waist. "I'll warn ya," she said.

The men around the tree were up and moving as the old man loaded Eddie into the truck.

Roy was surrounded by his friends. They all were congratulating him on the fight.

Preacher and Maggie watched from the background.

Hank had started toward Eddie at the same time Roy had stepped forward. He had slowed when Roy started speaking. He glanced over as Preacher stopped at Gene's side. He grinned when Roy's fist connected with Eddie's chin. Now he was watching Maggie. When she walked up to Preacher and looped her arm around his waist, he knew something had happened between the two of them. They looked like any other couple: comfortable.

Roy untangled himself from the group of men and headed toward Preacher. “Preacher,” Roy said, “thanks for the backup.”

Preacher smiled, “It didn’t look to me like you needed any.”

Roy sighed, “I was scared to death.”

Preacher beamed, “Son, there’s nothing wrong with being afraid; it’s what you do with that fear that counts. You did well.” Preacher offered his hand.

Roy shook it. “Preacher,” Roy continued, “would you mind helping me put Josh’s bed into the back of my truck?”

Tina spoke up, “I think Josh can sleep in your bed with me, and you can sleep on the couch. We’ll move the bed tomorrow.”

Roy laughed, “I’m not even married to her yet, and she’s already bossing me around.”

Maggie smiled. “She’s been bossing you around for years, Roy. You just didn’t know it.”

The party ended on a good note. Josh had awoke. He walked up the back pathway from Hank’s house, through the station, and discovered his blue BMX bike. He strode out from the station and stood in front of Preacher’s gleaming old girl. “Grandpa, Preacher fixed my bike. Mom says I can’t ride sheep for a while, but I can still ride my bike.”

Preacher applauded along with the crowd.

* * * * * * *

Everybody went home with food. Maggie insisted that Roy and Tina take home enough to last a day or two. Josh got the leftover cake. Charlie took a big plate of Preacher’s macaroni salad. Preacher commandeered Lupe’s Mexican bread.

The tables were cleaned and loaded. The chairs had been stacked back in Miguel’s truck. Preacher had policed the area himself. The party dwindled down to Hank, Maggie, and Preacher. Today had been a long one for the trio. The excitement of the party had drained the energy out of all of them.

“I’ll see you two later,” Hank said before he retired to his house to relax.

Preacher nodded.

"Preacher," Maggie stated, "thank you."

"Not a problem," he replied.

"Are you going to stay out here for awhile?" she asked.

"Yup."

Maggie smiled. "I'll be right back. I need to go check on Mom."

"I'll be right here," Preacher said as he ambled over to the tree.

Preacher sat under the old tree on the bench, smoking. He had a smile on his face. Tomorrow he would be back on the road. He still couldn't quite comprehend the significance of the delay. He believed that all things happened for a reason. He also believed that sometimes you had to take control of your destiny and do something. This road trip had a purpose. He felt an obligation.

* * * * * * *

Hank found Preacher in his bedroom packing. Preacher had pushed his bike back into the first bay and closed the door. He had rolled his laundry earlier. He had placed his saddle bags on his bed and was putting his socks in their proper place when Hank stepped into the room. He had already rolled up his sleeping bag.

"So…you're leaving in the morning?" Hank asked.

"Yup," he replied.

"You've caused quite a stir around here. Doing all my work, cleaning this place up, and solving our problem with Eddie."

Preacher looked over at Hank as he packed. "Eddie may still cause problems," he said.

Hank replied, "I think we can handle it. Eddie's a bully and a drunk. Now he's been whipped in front of all these people, I doubt he'll try much."

Preacher finished packing and stood up. "He might feel like he has to prove himself again."

"Then we'll have to whip him again," Hank said with a smile.

Picking up his saddle bags and sleeping bag, Preacher walked out to his bike. Hank followed.

"Some of these people would like you to stay, ya know," Hank said. He continued as Preacher started attaching the straps necessary to secure his load. "Frank talked to me about you working out of the station, working on equipment around here. I thought it was a good idea."

Preacher buckled his last strap. He stood up and met Hank's eyes. "Would you respect a man that didn't keep his word, Hank?"

"No."

"I gave my word to some of my brothers. I told them I would be at the Zion run a week from Saturday. I have two stops to make on my way. One stop is tomorrow night in Fillmore. I have to go, Hank; I gave my word."

Hank put his hands in his pockets. "Then I guess you have to go."

"That's right, I have to go," Preacher said as he started toward the front of the station. "Hank, I topped off my tanks," Preacher said over his shoulder.

"That's fine. I owe you more than a little gas," Hank said as he followed Preacher. "I was going to buy you a new tube, but I only had enough money for Maggie's flowers."

Preacher stopped and turned around. "Hank, you don't owe me anything. You helped a biker when you didn't have to. I just happened to be that biker. You bought me dinner and offered me a bed. It could have been any one of my brothers of the road. That's what we do when we're not working Hank, ride. Preacher stepped out into the crisp evening air. I'll let them know that this place is here. You can expect a lot more biker traffic. If you feel that you owe someone, help one of them when they need it."

Hank smiled, "Any *real* biker that comes through here can expect my help, cause he'll get it."

It was Preacher's turn to smile. "Do unto others," he said.

Hank nodded yes.

Maggie found them under the tree. "And how are my two favorite men doing?" she asked as she plopped down on the bench between the two of them.

Hank smiled. He leaned back against the tree. "It feels good to be home." He paused. "I hate hospitals."

Maggie turned toward him. "Hank," she asked, "do you want to talk about the money tonight?"

"No, not tonight. I think I just want to sit here and do nothing for a minute."

"Good," she said. "Because I didn't want to talk about it either." She sat back. "How did you like our party?" she asked.

Hank looked over and replied, "It was okay. I liked the part about Eddie the best."

Maggie sat back up. "I didn't expect Roy to stand up to Eddie. I thought it was going to be Preacher," she said. "He'd already knocked him down twice this morning."

Hank looked over at Preacher. "You forgot to mention that fact," he said.

"He was disrespectful," Preacher said still leaning back against the tree.

Hank looked back at Maggie. "I think this trip has changed a lot of things around here. Roy needs to step up. He's got a family to raise." Hank looked over at Preacher, "You'll miss the wedding."

"I don't like weddings," Preacher responded.

"Preacher!" Maggie snapped. "You don't want to see those two married?"

"Nope."

"Why?" she asked.

"I don't like weddings," he said.

Hank laughed. "Listen to yourselves. When did you two tie the knot?"

Preacher looked over at Hank. "Hank," he said, "I don't like weddings."

Maggie laughed. The trio stayed at the tree for a while. Maggie and Hank were gossiping, Preacher was listening.

The evening had started to cool down when Hank finally stood up and stretched. "Well, if you two don't mind, I think I'll go to bed. Now that I don't have Preacher to open up in the morning, I guess I'd better get some sleep." He looked at Preacher. "What time are you pulling out in the morning?" he asked.

Preacher responded without moving. "About forty-five minutes after Maggie's alarm goes off."

Maggie ducked her head and blushed.

Hank smiled. "Then I guess I'll see you two in the morning. Goodnight," he called over his shoulder as he ambled home.

Maggie leaned back against the tree. "Well, he took *that* quite well," she said.

"Maggie, he watched me pack."

"He still could have said something."

"He did," Preacher replied as he stood up and pulled Maggie to her feet. "Four-thirty comes early, girl. I need my sleep." He started toward the back of the diner.

"Don't count on too much sleep," she said as she caught up with him.

* * * * * * *

Preacher held the door when Maggie and he arrived at her back door. Maggie walked through the front room and turned right into the kitchen. Preacher followed.

"Do you have everything?" she asked as she prepared the coffee pot.

"I'm packed," Preacher said as he leaned against the door frame.

"I took some tea bags. I put them in my saddle bags," he said.

She turned from the counter. "That's fine; take whatever you need."

"I have," he replied.

She smiled, "Yeah, you have. It doesn't take much, does it, Preacher," she said.

"I've learned not to expect much."

"Oh, but you do expect a lot," she said.

"What do you mean by that?" he asked.

"Not many people could live by your code of honor," she stated.

"If it was easy, everybody would do it," he stated.

She shook her head. "You're something, Preacher," she said as she pushed away from the counter and extended her hand. "Come on, Romeo, let's go to bed. You need your rest, and you still have to satisfy me." She led the way into the bedroom.

Pillow talk was something Preacher had grown accustomed to during his stay with Maggie. She liked to cuddle. He held her in the crook of his arm. Preacher looked toward her and said, "If you ever need me, get a hold of Apache. You remember him?"

"Yes," she said.

"Good, I'll be in touch with him while I'm on this road trip. It might take a while for the road telegraph to work, but I will hear. I'll give you his card before I leave."

Maggie rose up on an elbow and asked, "How bad do I have to need you?"

Preacher chuckled. "If that Eddie character acts up again, definitely let Apache know. I *will* come back."

"Damn it," she said as she settled back down beside him.

* * * * * * *

Preacher woke with the alarm. Maggie stirred. Today was going to be a long, hard day, were Preacher's thoughts as he awoke. He had promised his cousin that he would stop by on his way to Zion. He had time, barring any flat tires.

Maggie stirred and rolled over to face Preacher. She looked at him, smiled, and said, "Every night and every morning, Preacher. I don't want it said that I'm not a woman of my word. That was our deal," she said with a smile.

"If I must," he said.

* * * * * * *

Maggie bounced out of bed and strolled into the kitchen. “Are you sure you have everything?” she asked as she turned on the coffee.

“I’ve been well taken care of,” Preacher replied from the bed.

Maggie walked back into the bedroom. “How long are you going to be on the road today?” she asked as she picked up the bedroom.

“Six, seven hours,” Preacher responded. He continued, “If I go tank to tank, I should make it sometime this afternoon.”

Casually she said, “Tell them I said ‘hello’.”

“I will,” Preacher said.

Maggie walked toward the bathroom. She turned around in the doorway and asked, “So....when are you coming back?”

“Maggie,” Preacher said in a stern voice.

“Well, when?” she asked.

“Every time I cross this country, I’ll stop. I have family in Utah. I make this trip at least twice a year. I just never stopped. I didn’t know you were here. Now, I’ll stop.”

“I knew you’d come back.”

“And how did you know that?” he asked.

Maggie stood in the doorway. With the lights behind her, she was a perfect silhouette. She struck a pose. With her legs spread, her hair brushed out, and her hands resting on the door frame, she said, “Once you’ve had the best.” She chuckled as she turned into the bathroom. “And make it more than a couple of times a year,” she said in a sassy voice.

Preacher smiled. He showered while Maggie got ready for work. He was brushing his hair out when he entered the kitchen. Maggie wasn’t wearing her normal uniform. Today, she was in her Levi’s. She stood facing the sink. “What do you want for breakfast?” she asked over her shoulder.

“Oatmeal,” he said.

“Oatmeal?” she asked.

“Yeah, with brown sugar and raisins.”

She looked over at him and said, “You and your sweet tooth.”

“Oatmeal will stay with me for a while.”

"Good," she said as she started to prepare his meal. "If you'll sit down, I'll braid your hair," she said.

He sat at the table. "I noticed you're not wearing your uniform this morning."

Maggie walked up behind him. "What Hank said last night got me to thinking. There's more than my uniform that needs to be changed around here," she said as she started on Preacher's hair.

"And what would those changes be?" he asked.

"I'm not wearing a uniform anymore. And I'm not putting my hair up in that awful bun. I own this place. I've worked hard to get the business I have. These people will notice, but I don't think they'll care. They all know I've been with you. They all know and respect you. There are a couple of changes I'm going to make."

"A change is good sometimes," he responded.

"Some things never change," she said pulling his hair a little too tight.

"You're right," he said.

"There," she said as she finished his warrior braid. She turned back to the stove for his breakfast. "Here," she said as she dished it up. "You've got a long day ahead of you. Eat." She sat down across from him. "Will you do something for me?" she asked. She continued, "Call me when you get to your cousin's?"

"I don't have your number."

"I'll give it to you before you leave. Will you do something else?"

Preacher looked up at her. "What is it, something that hurts you, or something you can't see?"

Maggie sat up. "What?" she said.

"The last time somebody asked me to do something, it cost me a week," Preacher said.

Maggie laughed. "No, it's not my brakes, but I would like a postcard from time to time."

Preacher resumed eating. "I don't have your address," he said between spoonfuls of the sweet oatmeal.

Maggie smiled. It was fun to banter with Preacher. "Okay," she said. "I'll give you a list: my phone number, my address, and my birthday."

Preacher finished eating. Dropping his spoon into the empty bowl, he looked up with a smile. "Why would I want to know your birthday?" he asked.

"So you can send me a card and call me." She was smiling as she sat back, proud of herself.

"We'll see," he said as he got up and placed his bowl in the sink. "It's time to go, Maggie," he said.

She looked up, "I know," she said. "I'll write your list and bring it over." She looked up at him.

Preacher looked down at her; he patted her head, "You're a good woman, Maggie," he said.

She abruptly stood up. "Preacher," she stomped her foot, "I'd better get more than a pat on the head." She did.

He laughed.

* * * * * * *

Hank heard the bay door open. He had been standing at the front window when Preacher crossed the highway and walked through the back of the station. The sun was not up yet, but the false dawn had thrown shadows. He was glad that Preacher and Maggie had enjoyed each other's company. Maggie needed that from time to time. He smiled. I'll bet she doesn't go to Fallon for a while, he thought as he walked out the back door and proceeded up the gravel path.

Hank stepped through the back door in time to see Preacher push his bike out the front; both bike and rider were black. He knew Preacher was encased in black leather.

Preacher pushed his bike out to the pumps and put down the kick stand. He opened one of his saddle bags. He took out a card or something. After putting it in his scrodie pocket, he began to snap and zip his leather together.

Hank looked up as Maggie walked over from the diner. She wasn't wearing her uniform, and her hair was down. She walked up to Preacher. "Here's the list. Stay in touch, will ya?" she asked as she handed him a piece of paper. Hank started forward.

"Here's the card for Apache. I meant it when I said if that Eddie jerk causes any trouble, I want to know."

She nodded. "I'll let you know," she said.

Hank walked up. "So, you were going to leave and not say goodbye?" he asked.

Preacher turned around, smiled, and offered his hand. "Hank, I don't say 'goodbye', I say 'see ya when I see ya'."

Hank took his hand and said, "That works for me."

Preacher secured his helmet and straddled his old girl. He looked up at Maggie. "If you ever need me, you know how," he said as he pulled on his gloves. The sun was breaking the horizon to the east.

Maggie touched his arm. "Have a safe run," she said.

"I'll try," Preacher said as he hit the starter button. The old girl roared to life, then settled into the heartbeat of an old '74. He put on his glasses. "See ya when I see ya," he said as he clicked down once and released the clutch.

Maggie and Hank stood side by side as they watched Preacher disappear into the sunrise. The sun was only halfway up the horizon. What they saw was the black silhouette of him on his bike with his arms extended up to the ape hangers, shimmering into the rising sun. Hank put his hands in his pockets. "Do you think he'll ever be back?" he asked.

Maggie smiled. "He said, 'when I see ya', didn't he? He'll be back."

Hank said, "If he ever does come back, he'll always have a bed and meal."

Maggie chuckled and looked over at Hank. "When he does come back, he won't be sleeping in that squeaky old bed."

Hank looked over at her with a knowing smile. "And how do you know that bed squeaks?" he asked.

Maggie took her stance, shook her head, and said, "History, Hank, history."

Maggie strolled toward the diner. It was almost time to open. She still had biscuits to make. Oh well, she thought, it'll get done, sometime.

Hank watched Maggie cross the highway. It's amazing what a simple flat tire can turn into, were his thoughts. He started toward the station to close the bay door. He didn't have to open for two more hours. He would have coffee with Maggie. Today was another day.

## Epilogue
## Ten Days Later

At five o'clock in the afternoon, the sun showed no mercy for the audience of the local rodeo. The golden orb shone down with all its brilliance. The color guard had made their entrance, and the national anthem had been sung. Roy, Josh, and Hank occupied the seats directly in front of Tina and Maggie. It was time for the mutton bustin'.

Josh had anxiously awaited the event. He knew that if he could ride, he would win. He had critiqued the first contestant.

"Mom, I could beat him," he said. Hank and Roy agreed.

"You'll show them next year, son," Roy responded.

Tina glanced over at Maggie. "Have you heard anything from Preacher yet? He ought to be in Zion by now," she said.

"Yes," Maggie said. "I got a postcard from him today. It was postmarked Wednesday."

"Well, I got a bit of unusual news when I got home yesterday," Tina said. She continued, "I called the hospital and talked to the financial assistance people. They said that the bill had been paid in full."

Maggie hesitated before she turned to face Tina. "Are you sure? There must be a mistake."

Tina continued, "That's what I thought. I asked them to check."

Maggie was excited, "Well?" she said.

"They told me that a lawyer with long gray hair came in and paid it."

"What?" Maggie screamed.

"They said that a guy by the name of Daymond came in, identified himself, and paid the bill."

Maggie cocked her head. "Are you sure?" she asked.

"That's what they told me."

"I'd check on that if I were you," Maggie said. "That doesn't sound right. Unless you have an angel on your shoulder, that just doesn't happen."

Tina shook her head. “I couldn’t believe it. I asked them to check. They said that the bill was paid.” Tina paused. “I don’t know what to think. I haven’t said anything to Roy yet.”

Roy turned around. “What haven’t you told me?” he asked.

Tina smiled. “Watch the rodeo, cowboy; we’ll discuss it later.”

“Okay,” he said as he turned back around.

Josh spoke up with conviction. “I’ll show them next year.”

Roy looked at his soon-to-be stepson. “Damn bet you will. Next year you’ll show them how it’s done,” he commented.

Tina looked back at Maggie.

“I asked to talk to the supervisor. She told me that this guy Daymond came in, asked for Josh’s billing, negotiated on some of the charges, then gave them a certified check for over two hundred and fifty thousand dollars. She said she remembered because it doesn’t happen very often. She asked who the benefactor was. She said he just smiled and walked out.”

Maggie stared at Tina for a moment. “I can’t think of anybody with that kind of money. It must be a charity or something.”

“I don’t know what or who, but I’d sure like to meet the people involved. I’d name our next child after them.”

Maggie laughed. “You’re not even married yet, and you’re already planning another child?”

Tina blushed, “Roy wants a daughter.”

Maggie smiled, “I guess you could always call her Charity,” she said.

Tina laughed.

Maggie sat back in thought. “Tina,” she said, “do you remember what Preacher was always saying about doing unto others?”

“Yes, yes I do,” Tina responded.

Maggie looked off into space. “Well, I think you owe somebody a lot of kindness.”

***Excerpt from book two in the series:***

Preacher mingled with the brothers. He ate a hotdog, but he drank tea. Preacher would have a beer once in awhile, after a hard day's work in the sun, but he preferred his tea. He stood chatting with a friend when the young hang-around showed back up.

"Dale, who is that kid? He's been watching me all night long."

Dale looked over at the young up-start. "I don't know his name, but he's always around. He doesn't say much, but he rides. I've seen him a couple of times by himself. I don't think he's trouble. Want me to ask?"

"If you wouldn't mind. I'd appreciate it."

"Sure," Dale replied.

* * * * * * *

George and Preacher were sitting on the porch when Dale walked up. "Preacher, I think you have a new hang-around. He asked a couple of discreet questions about you."

Preacher offered Dale a chair with a wave of his hand. "What kind of questions?"

Dale sat down. "Who you're affiliated with, and where you're going."

Preacher smiled. He knew that if you asked a question, and it really wasn't any of your business, bikers wouldn't tell you. "Is he getting any answers?" he asked.

Dale smiled, "No."

"Good," Preacher responded.

Dale looked over at Preacher. "Where are you going?" he asked.

Preacher smiled. "Denver."

Dale sat back. "Would you deliver a package for me?"

"Sure," Preacher responded. "Where am I taking it?" he asked.

Dale smiled, “Probably the same place you’re going. The clubhouse.”

“That works for me. I’ll be leaving the day after tomorrow, early.”

Dale nodded his head. “I’ll have it here for you tomorrow.”

The kid strolled by.

“Hey, kid,” Preacher hollered. The kid looked over. “Me?” he asked.

Preacher waved his hand. “Yeah, you. Come here.”

The kid put his hands in his pockets as he walked up to the porch. “Yes, sir?” he asked.

Preacher smiled. The kid was respectful. He liked that. “Do you have any papers?”

The kid beamed, “Yes, sir,” as he reached into his cut-off Levi jacket and retrieved a pack. He offered them to Preacher.

“No, I want you to roll me a smoke,” Preacher said. He slid his hand into his scrodie and produced the makings.

“Sure, the kid said as he took a bud and started breaking it up. Dale, George, and Preacher watched. His hands shook. When he was through, he handed Preacher back the smallest pinner he had ever seen. He smiled.

“You keep that for yourself. Now roll me a good one.”

“Sorry,” he said.

This time the kid took his time and produced a nice round cigarette.

“That’s better, Preacher said as he handed the doobie to Dale. Sit down for a minute. I want to talk to you.”

“Yes, sir,” the kid said as he sat down.

“I understand you are asking questions about me. Don’t you think it might be a good idea to ask me instead of sneaking around?”

“Sorry,” he said.

“And quit saying ‘I’m sorry.’ Never say you are sorry.”

The kid nodded his head.

“Okay,” Preacher sat back. “Now ask.”

“Well, sir, I was just wondering where you were going.”

"Why?"

"Cause I was thinking of asking if I could ride along with you."

Preacher sat up. "Why would you want to ride with me? You have some damn good people right here to ride with."

"Utah doesn't fit me. I always feel out of place. I was thinking that if I went with you, I might find a place to call home."

Preacher studied the kid. "Does it matter where I'm going?"

"No, sir. I have a poncho liner on my bike and a couple pair of clean socks in my saddle bags."

Preacher looked to the right at George. "Can you believe this?"

George was smiling. "He has all the right answers."

Preacher looked to the left at Dale. "What do you think? he asked.

Dale was grinning. "If he fucks up, you could always kick him to the curb."

Preacher looked back at the kid. "Plan on staying here tomorrow night. We'll leave at sunrise."

* * * * * * *

The day after the party was overcast. The first part of June, in Utah, could still get cold at night. Preacher remembered his grandfather telling him, "You never plant your vegetable garden until Memorial Day. It could still freeze." It hadn't gotten that cold during the night, but the morning air had been brisk. Preacher had run some errands for supplies. George had cleaned up around his house. Dale showed up around two in the afternoon and had left around four. Preacher was packing away his acquisitions when the kid showed up. It made him smile.

When the kid pulled up into George's yard, Preacher likened it to Jed Clampett's arrival in Beverly Hills. It looked like he had packed everything he owned, including the kitchen sink, on the back and front of his old bike. Preacher called back to George. "George, you might want to come out and see this. It's a sight to behold."

George ambled out onto the porch. "Where's he think he's going? Tennessee?" It had been too dark the night before to take a good look at any of the bikes. Preacher had certainly missed this one. The kid's bike was an old '75 FLH. It looked like it was mostly original. The wide glide front end and the ape hangers shone in the evening sun. The frame, fat bobs, and rear fender were painted rattle-can semi-gloss black. His motor and transmission were spotless. His seat had been re-covered. A poncho liner wrapped around a tool pouch and what looked like a telescoping fishing rod adorned the place behind his headlight. His well used black saddle bags bulged. A duffle bag wrapped with a low-dollar blue tarp occupied the rear seat. The bungee cords that held it in place also secured a small coffee pot and frying pan. The kid was ready to travel.

He was a good looking kid. He stood six feet tall with a medium frame. His arms and shoulders were muscled. His face was young but held the wisdom of someone who had taken care of himself for awhile. His long black hair was pulled back into a braid that hung well below his shoulder blades. George and Preacher strolled out to greet him.

"Well, kid, it looks like you're ready to travel," Preacher said as they strolled up. "Did you have to bring everything you own?"

The kid looked up defiantly. "Yes, sir. I don't plan on coming back."

Preacher smiled. He liked this kid already. "Okay," he said. "You're packing it."

The kid crawled off his bike. "I won't be holding you back; if I do, just keep going. I'll catch up."

Preacher looked sideways at him. "Remember you said that. I'll hold you to it."

The kid flushed. He knew he had acted cocky. "Yes, sir," he said.

Preacher nodded his head. "Did you take care of all your business and say all your goodbyes?"

"Yes, sir."

"Good," Preacher said. "Come on up to the house. I bought us all steaks for tonight, and George agreed to cook them. It's the last good meal we're going to get for a couple of days."

"Yes, sir," the kid replied.

LaVergne, TN USA
16 October 2009

161161LV00001B/41/A

9 781601 450586